CHECKMATE

CHRONICLES OF NEW BHARAT

ALOK SHAH

notionpress
.com

INDIA • SINGAPORE • MALAYSIA

Author's Disclaimer

Within the pages of *Checkmate: Chronicles of New Bharat*, the characters and events are products of artistic interpretation and creative liberty. While there might be reflections or echoes of historical figures or events, they have been repurposed for the narrative. This work is fictional, and any parallels to real individuals, living or deceased, or actual events are purely coincidental. This book is intended solely for the reader's engagement and reflection, and I urge readers to approach it with discernment, recognizing the boundary between fact and fiction. The intention is never to misrepresent or offend but to offer a narrative exploration. Your understanding is appreciated.

Summary

In a reimagined India, Cyrus Engineer, an unassuming Parsi leader, is unexpectedly made the first prime minister, steering the nation into an era of tumult and transformation. With a backdrop of political subterfuge, international intrigue, and historic alliances, the narrative delves deep into the dynamics of power and the nuances of diplomacy. As Cyrus navigates covert alliances, contentious decisions, and domestic challenges, India's very fabric is tested. *Checkmate: Chronicles of New Bharat* is a suspense-filled alternate history tale, questioning loyalties, motives, and the true essence of power in the world's largest democracy. As tensions rise, mysteries unravel, alliances are forged and broken, and India's destiny hangs in the balance. Who's playing whom, and who will declare the checkmate in the end?

Blurb

In a world of shadows and secrets, Cyrus Engineer, an unassuming Parsi, is thrust into the highest office of India. As he grapples with unexpected power dynamics, old allegiances, and emerging conspiracies, one question looms large: Who truly holds the power in this new Bharat? When the fate of a newly born nation transforms into a high-stakes game on a grand chessboard, every move is laced with suspense and mystery. Unexpected allies, hidden motives, and international machinations converge in this intricate thriller. In the sprawling labyrinth of New Bharat's politics, can Prime Minister Engineer discern friend from foe? Dive into the *Chronicles of New Bharat* and uncover the enigma. The board is set, the pieces are moving. Who will claim victory in this riveting game of strategy and subterfuge?

CONTENTS

PREFACE

In *Checkmate: The Chronicles of New Bharat*, the line between the real and the imaginary often blurs. It is essential to understand that this work aims not to substitute historical records but to supplement our imagination—to offer a lens through which we might see what could have been if certain variables were tweaked.

The characters I've crafted in this narrative—Cyrus, Dharmadhikari, Gokhale, and others—represent not just individuals but ideas. They are embodiments of the conflicts, aspirations, and hopes that marked that crucial period in Indian history. Through their struggles and triumphs, I've tried to explore the intricate dance between personal ambitions and national duty, the tensions that arise when tradition confronts modernity, and the age-old debate between determinism and free will.

As you embark on this journey, you will encounter familiar landmarks and historical figures, yet the course of events might deviate from what you know or expect. This is the beauty of alternative history—it allows us to imagine a world of infinite possibilities while remaining anchored to a core set of known truths.

I've always believed that while history teaches us about our past, fiction allows us to dream, to wonder, and to challenge the status quo. This book is my humble attempt to merge the two, to create a narrative that is as engaging as it is enlightening.

I would like to thank the countless historians, scholars, and writers who have documented the events of 1947 and the years that followed. Their meticulous work has provided the canvas upon which I've painted this story. My gratitude also extends to the many people who shared their stories and memories with me, offering invaluable insights into the era.

Before delving into the intricacies of this narrative, I must pause and acknowledge the invaluable contributions of those who stood by me during the creation of this work. My deepest gratitude goes to my entire family, especially my life partner, for her unconditional love and support. Through long nights and countless revisions, they were my anchors. Their unwavering patience and understanding during this journey were nothing short of extraordinary. It was their faith in me, and the countless cups of coffee they provided, that kept me going even when the words seemed elusive. To them, I owe this story and so much more.

Lastly, to you, dear reader, thank you for embarking on this journey with me. Whether you agree or disagree with the turns this narrative takes, I hope it provokes thought, stimulates debate, and most importantly, keeps the flame of curiosity alive.

Here's to the past that was, the present that is, and the myriad futures that might have been.

With deepest gratitude,

Alok Shah

Chapter 1

NEW DAWN

August 15, 1947, 2:00 p.m.: The Governor General's Residence, New Delhi

The dry wind carried the whispers of thousands. A sea of people gathered to witness history unfold. Their attention was fixated on a figure emerging from the massive assembly hall gates, moving towards the podium with a shroud of trepidation. This wasn't the man they had come to see, the leader they had been rallying behind all these years.

With his dapper Parsi-style suit, Cyrus Engineer adjusted his spectacles and cleared his throat. The weight of a nation's hopes pressed down on him. The air was thick with anticipation and surprise.

The vast halls of the governor general's palace echoed with the footsteps of leaders and dignitaries. The grand edifice, built by the British, had seen many a ceremony, but today, there was an electrifying tension in the air.

Cyrus stood near the opulent French windows, his face a calm mask but his heart racing. The sheer stress of the office he was about to assume seemed to suffocate him. His eyes flitted across the room, capturing moments: the curious glances of the foreign diplomats, the expectant looks of the press, the uncertain whispers among the political elites. Each gaze and murmur only added to the cacophony in his mind.

His hand trembled slightly as he adjusted his tie for the umpteenth time. He was snapped out of his thoughts by a gentle hand on his shoulder.

Cyrus stepped forward, his heart pounding but his face a mask of determination. The room descended into a thick silence, pierced only by the distant call of a bird outside.

Lord Williamson gestured to Cyrus to raise his hand. "Raise your hand up for an oath and repeat after me."

Drawing a deep breath, Cyrus placed his right hand on the tome. The expectations of his predecessors, the dreams of millions, and the hope of a unified future pressed into his palm.

"I, Cyrus Engineer," he began, his voice carrying through the hall.

"I, Cyrus Engineer," echoed Lord Williamson, ensuring the gravity of the moment wasn't lost.

"Do solemnly swear," Cyrus continued, "that I will bear true faith and allegiance to the newly independent India."

"That I will uphold the sovereignty and integrity of our great nation. That I will faithfully and conscientiously discharge my duties as the prime minister for all its people, irrespective of caste, creed, religion, or region."

"That I shall preserve, protect, and defend the sovereignty and the laws of the nation, and that I shall devote myself to the service and well-being of the people of India."

As he finished his oath, a wave of emotion swept through the room. The gravity of the promise, the hope pinned on his shoulders, and the challenges that lay ahead were all palpable. And yet, in that room, the birth of a new India, under the leadership of a young Parsi named Cyrus Engineer was celebrated with fervent hope and collective aspiration.

But the unease refused to settle. Flashbacks of the journey to this day raced through Cyrus's mind. Was he truly ready? Would the nation accept a leader who wasn't elected through conventional means?

As the governor general's aide signalled for the ceremony to commence, a chilling thought crossed Cyrus's mind. *What if this is a mistake? What if this very hall, with its grandeur and legacy, witnesses my undoing?*

His heartbeat seemed to synchronize with the ceremonial drums that now began to beat, announcing the commencement of the oath-taking ceremony. The ambient conversations were hushed, replaced by the almost surreal hum of anticipation.

The governor general, standing tall and regal, beckoned him forward. Each step felt like an eternity. The luxurious red carpet beneath seemed to shift like quicksand, making every stride a challenge.

But Cyrus, drawing from an inner reservoir of strength, took the final step. He met the governor general's gaze, his own eyes now steely with determination. The very room that threatened to be his undoing now bore witness to his resolve.

As the oath echoed through the hall, binding him to the service of the nation, Cyrus felt a transformation. The weight, instead of dragging him down, now seemed to anchor him and give him purpose.

The ceremony concluded amidst thunderous applause. The tension had not dissipated, but it had transformed. It was now the tension of a new beginning, of a journey that had just commenced, and of a leader who had been tested in the fire of his doubts and emerged stronger.

"I stand here," Cyrus began, voice quivering, "as your prime minister, not by ambition but by circumstance."

The crowd looked on, a mix of reverence, uncertainty, and whispers. Among the whispers, a few faces stood out.

As the oath concluded, Cyrus, surrounded by a bevy of officials and bodyguards, was ushered hurriedly into the governor general's quarters.

The governor general's quarter stood tall, draped in the tricolour, symbolizing the dawn of a new era. People from all walks of life had gathered, their eyes glistening with tears, pride, and hope.

Amid the sea of people, Cyrus stood, his heart swelling with pride. But his thoughts weren't just centred on the present. He thought about the sacrifices, the struggles, the sheer tenacity it had taken to reach this day. He glanced around, soaking in the atmosphere, locking this memory deep within his heart.

August 13, 1947: The Engineer Residence, Forty-Eight Hours Prior to the Oath-Taking Ceremony, Bombay

The steady drumming of rain outside draped a serene façade over the luxurious bungalow that stood regally, gazing out towards the Arabian Sea. Inside, a tall, broad-shouldered man, Cyrus, was sipping his evening tea, deep in discussion with a petite, fair-skinned woman with striking blue eyes.

At 33 years old, he was the epitome of a young, intellectual Parsi, his life marked by privilege, education, and a lineage of philanthropy. The spacious room, adorned with tasteful art and symbols of rich heritage, reflected the life and legacy he was born into. With his sharp features and dark eyes often hidden behind spectacles, Cyrus carried the air of someone who had navigated the halls of academia with ease. His tall, lean frame and the way he held himself spoke of a life lived amidst culture and intellectual pursuit.

"Cyrus," Richelle his British-born wife began, breaking the comfortable silence, "you seem miles away. What's on your mind?" Her voice was soft yet carried a note of curiosity. She was familiar with his often introspective moods.

Cyrus looked up, meeting her gaze. "Just reflecting," he replied, his voice tinged with nostalgia. "On Oxford, on the Labour Party… on Father." His years at Oxford had been a transformative experience, widening his perspectives on political science and world affairs. His subsequent involvement with the Labour Party in the UK had given him a taste of practical politics, an internship experience that he had treasured. Richelle brushed back her golden hair, staring at the map spread out before them. "The cottage by the Thames sounds lovely. Our future children would love it, don't you think?"

A deep sigh escaped Cyrus. "Yes, Richelle. Leaving behind the politics, the chaos… it's all I've been dreaming about."

In the candle-lit corners of their ancestral home, adorned with Indian antiques and age-old paintings, Cyrus found a rare moment of peace with Richelle. The crackling noise of the gramophone in the background played an old English tune, reminiscent of the Raj and the British influence in India.

Richelle sat in the embrace of an intricately carved wooden chair, her fingers fidgeting with a British penny she had acquired during one of the recent visits by British delegates. "So, Cyrus," she began, her voice soft yet filled with anticipation, "once this turbulence settles, we'll finally be moving to London. Imagine, the city which is at the heart of this empire. We'll get to experience it first-hand."

Cyrus, his eyes reflecting a blend of excitement and apprehension, responded, "It took endless nights and countless discussions to convince my family members. Given their philanthropic roots, and their dedication to India, they were reluctant. But I made them see our aspirations, our desire to witness the world beyond. London after the war and now on the cusp of losing its crown jewel—India. It will be a changed world, and I want us to be a part of it."

She looked up, the candlelight catching the glint in her eyes. "The theatres, the cobblestone streets, the art... It's a new chapter, Cyrus. But tell me, do you think we'll ever truly belong there? Or will we always be remnants of this departing Raj?"

Cyrus took a deep breath. "We're venturing into an evolving world, Richelle. London post-war, India gaining independence... it's a world reshaping its identity. As for us, our roots are here, but our dreams are there. We'll find our place."

Richelle's gaze returned to the penny in her hand, symbolizing the empire that had ruled them and the city that awaited them. The future seemed uncertain, but it held the promise of adventure, growth, and discovery.

Cyrus's return to India during his internship in London had been abrupt, driven by the unexpected loss of his father. The patriarch of the Engineer family had been more than just a successful businessman; he was a respected philanthropist and an advisor to the Indian National Party. His passing had left a void, not just in Cyrus's life but in the many social initiatives he supported,

Cyrus, amidst the elegant surroundings that spoke of his family's wealth and taste, was at a pivotal crossroads. His decision to leave India again to go back to England, just six years after his return, was not made lightly but with a considered understanding of what the future could hold.

He had spent the past few months meticulously planning this transition. Understanding the responsibilities tied to his family's extensive business interests, Cyrus had taken great care in appointing a team of loyal and trustworthy family members. These were individuals he knew could handle the diverse and expansive operations with the same dedication and acumen his father had shown. His choices were strategic, ensuring that each sector of the business was under capable stewardship.

In his heart, Cyrus felt a sense of relief and accomplishment. He believed he had successfully set up a structure that would allow the business to flourish even in his absence. This reassurance was crucial for him, as it meant his departure to the UK wouldn't disrupt the legacy his father had built. As the sun bowed out, casting long shadows over the manicured lawns, the rhythmic thumping of leather boots reached a crescendo. Vehicles, reminiscent of the British military but now bearing the nascent symbols of soon-to-be independent India, pulled up with an abruptness that sent plumes of dust into the evening air.

Before they could fathom what was transpiring, the wooden doors to his study were thrown open, revealing a phalanx of guards. Their crisp khakis and turbans symbolized a new India, but their demeanour was that of the old world.

"You're needed immediately," declared their sergeant, urgency clear in his voice.

Taken aback but sensing the gravity, Cyrus asked, "Might I know the reason for this abrupt summons?"

"There's no time, sir. It's a directive from the top brass," came the swift reply.

Quickly, they escorted him through the sprawling corridors of his ancestral home. The convoy, led by a vintage Rolls Royce now adorned with the tricolour, made its way through the winding streets of Bombay, the once familiar British landmarks now viewed under the fresh lens of freedom.

They stopped at Bombay Airport. An aircraft, one of those recently handed over by the departing British, stood prepped for take-off. The engines' drone seemed to mirror the throbbing pulse of the nation in transition.

"Delhi awaits, sir. All will be revealed at the governor general's residence," the sergeant whispered, his voice barely audible over the roar of the propellers.

"You're summoned by Lord Williamson in Delhi. Immediately!" The officer looked neither apologetic nor accommodating.

The plane hummed, steadily cutting through the monsoon-laden skies of August. The flight was a luxury, not afforded to many in 1947. With mixed emotions, Cyrus peered out of the window, watching the patchwork of the Indian landscape slowly change beneath him. The proximity of India's independence, a dream for many and soon to be a reality, filled the atmosphere with palpable tension.

Lost in his thoughts, he was interrupted by the rustle of a newspaper. Glancing to his side, he saw a tall, imposing figure settling into the seat next to him. This man was unmistakably British, with sharp aquiline features, silver-grey hair impeccably combed back, and an immaculate moustache that signified a military background. His tailored suit, crisply ironed, and shining shoes all screamed of a man who adhered strictly to protocol.

"Lord Williamson," the man introduced himself, extending a hand, which Cyrus shook.

Cyrus had heard of him. Lord Williamson was the last governor general of India. He had been serving in various administrative positions in the United Kingdom for the last two decades. He was known to be a stern administrator and a stickler for rules but also fair in his dealings. Stories of his wit, and sometimes, unpredictable decisions were widely discussed in bureaucratic circles.

"What's going on?" Cyrus asked, his voice laced with concern.

Taking a deep breath, Lord Williamson's voice revealed, "Cyrus, you're to be our interim prime minister."

Stunned, Cyrus tried to process the words. "What? How?"

Williamson leaned back in his seat, adjusting his spectacles. "Ah, the questions of destiny. Let me tell you, young man, positions of leadership are often thrust upon those who least expect it."

"But why me? It doesn't make sense," Cyrus pressed, seeking answers.

Lord Williamson chuckled softly. "Life rarely offers straightforward answers. But rest assured, you will have all your questions answered in due time. India stands at a crossroads. It needs leaders, not just politicians. Perhaps those who chose you saw something in you that even you're unaware of."

Throughout the flight, Cyrus's initial question lingered, only to be punctuated by Lord Williamson's cryptic assurance that answers would come.

The journey was not just a physical movement from one place to another for Cyrus—it was the beginning of his introspection into the role destiny had chosen for him. The encounter with Lord Williamson was not just a chance meeting but a stepping stone to understanding the path that lay ahead.

As the flight continued, what could have been an uncomfortable journey became an insightful dialogue between two men—one representing the colonial past and the other the hopeful future of a nation on the cusp of rebirth.

August 15, 1947, Noon: The Governor General's Residence… Two Hours before Oath-Taking, New Delhi

Cyrus sat in a grand room, surrounded by the titans of the era with Lord Williamson, observing his every reaction. As Cyrus settled into the grand drawing room, the elegant double doors swung open with a flourish. A dignified figure, with grace and stature that commanded immediate attention, walked in. Panditji, as he was respectfully addressed by most, was a vision of traditional elegance. He wore a finely woven, pristine white kurta-pyjama, over which was draped a light pashmina shawl, hinting at the early winter chill outside.

His skin, tanned by years under the sun during the freedom movement, was a stark contrast to his snow-white attire. With piercing dark eyes set beneath a prominent brow, his gaze was both intense and kind, reflecting the wisdom of someone who had seen and lived through a great deal. His thin lips, often breaking into a warm smile, sat below a sharply angular nose. Thin silver strands peeked through his neatly tied-back hair, symbolizing the battles he had fought and the maturity he had gained from them.

His voice, deep and measured, echoed with authority but without arrogance. "Cyrus," he began, nodding slightly, his eyes fixed on the young man in front of him, "it's been a while."

Cyrus, despite being caught off guard by his sudden elevation to prime minister, felt a strange sense of comfort in Panditji's presence. This was a man who had overseen the birth of a nation, and Cyrus knew he was in safe hands.

As Cyrus and Panditji exchanged greetings in the grand drawing room, the doors opened once more, revealing two more figures who were as integral to India's tapestry as Panditji himself.

The first to step in was Patel Sahib. A robust man, built like a banyan tree—wide, sturdy, and grounded. He had the air of someone who didn't just witness history but actively moulded it. His skin was sun-kissed, reflecting the long hours he had spent in rural India uniting various princely states. Dressed in a traditional dhoti and kurta, with a shawl draped over one shoulder, he had a charisma that was unmistakably rustic yet refined. His broad forehead was adorned with a prominent tilak, symbolizing his deep roots in Hindu traditions. His eyes were sharp, often giving away little, yet anyone who gazed into them could see the flames of passion for a united India. With a thick, greying moustache crowning his mouth, his entire countenance was that of a man who would stand resolute in the face of any adversity.

Following closely behind was Ali Bhai, contrasting Patel Sahib in many ways yet equally compelling. He was slender and of medium height with an olive complexion, reflecting his Pathan lineage. His attire was an impeccable sherwani, capped with a well-fitted fez, representing the sophistication of the Muslim nobility of the time. His deep-set eyes sparkled with intelligence and often had a mischievous glint. They were the eyes of a master strategist. His beard, neatly trimmed, gave him an air of aristocratic elegance. But beyond his physical appearance, it was his aura of calm and deep understanding of India's diverse communities that set him apart. He was a bridge between contrasting worlds, someone who could bring unity in diversity.

As they stepped forward, the room transformed into a tableau of India's leading lights, each representing a facet of this vast nation.

Panditji, with his wise old eyes, looked equally concerned and assured. Patel, statesman of the Indian National Party, and Ali Bhai, leader of the Muslim Quam, all focused on the newly appointed leader.

Panditji explained, "Cyrus, we're at a juncture where India cannot afford partition. The Empire, our brethren from the Muslim Quam, and we of the Indian National Party have found a middle ground. You, being neither Hindu nor Muslim, and with a history of brokering peace, will be our interim prime minister till the Constitution is framed."

Cyrus looked at them incredulously. "But my experience… it's not—"

Lord Williamson interrupted, "It's exactly what India needs. Fresh perspective. Neutral stance."

Ali Bhai leaned forward. "You were chosen for a reason, Engineer. The people trust neutrality and your family's dedication to this nation."

Lord Williamson nodded in agreement. "Yes, and aside from your own merit, the legacy of your father—one of India's greatest philanthropists— lends an undeniable credibility to your leadership. Your family has always put India before any religious or regional ties. This is not just about selecting a leader but also about sending a message of unity to every corner of the nation."

"And you'll not be alone," Panditji continued. "Patel, Ali Bhai, and I will form an advisory committee."

Cyrus looked up at Panditji, Patel Sahib, and Ali Bhai, each standing in the room, observing his every reaction.

"How is this even possible?" Cyrus began, his voice tinged with disbelief. "Last I remember, I was nowhere near the political radar. And overnight, I find myself the leader of this nation. Aren't the stalwarts of the Muslim Quam and the Indian National Party incensed? How can there not be opposition or rebellion?"

Panditji exchanged glances with Ali Bhai before the latter pulled out an official-looking document from his briefcase. It was a memorandum, with signatures densely packed on both sides of the parchment.

"Sometimes, circumstances demand radical decisions," Panditji began, his voice serene. "While the path was fraught with debates and disagreements, the leaders of both the Muslim Quam and the Indian National Party have signed this memorandum. It demonstrates their support for you, Cyrus, as the next prime minister."

Cyrus took the document in his hands, his fingers grazing over the myriad signatures. Names of political leaders, some familiar, others not so much, stared back at him. His heart raced, the magnitude of what lay in his hands not lost on him.

"But... why? Why me?" Cyrus stammered, looking up to meet the gazes of the three men.

Ali Bhai cleared his throat. "The nation needed a symbol of unity, someone who isn't entrenched in the usual political mudslinging and who is neither Hindu nor Muslim. Your name came up as that beacon. A beacon that signifies hope, change, and a fresh start. It is the legacy of your Parsi heritage, your lineage of neutrality and philanthropy, that had made you the singular unifying choice acceptable to both the Indian National Party and the Muslim Quam. Your father's legacy of bridge-building between communities, of being a voice of reason and moderation in tumultuous times, had unwittingly cast you into this decisive role."

"Cyrus, the choice before you is stark and immediate," Lord Williamson intervened, his voice steady yet tinged with a hint of regret. "Accept the mantle of prime ministership or witness the division of this nation into two separate entities—India and Pakistan. Time is a luxury we do not possess; I have orders to complete the transfer of power by the 15th of August."

The air was thick with tension, the magnitude of the decision hanging like a sword over the room. Cyrus, still reeling from the abrupt turn his life had taken, felt the pressure mount. The walls, lined with portraits of past viceroys, seemed to bear down upon him, their eyes fixed in a silent, collective stare.

Before Cyrus could respond, Ali Bhai interjected, his voice carrying a grave note that underscored the severity of the situation. "There is, I fear, a third possible outcome should you decline," he said solemnly. "A civil war that could tear the very fabric of our nation."

The room fell into a hushed silence, the words 'civil war' echoing ominously. Cyrus, standing at the precipice of history, felt the full burden of his decision. It was not just about his future but the destiny of millions. The enormity of centuries of history, of the hopes and aspirations of a subjugated people, now rested on his shoulders.

Cyrus sat back, attempting to process everything. The room, with all its grandeur and history, seemed to close in on him, but the presence of these seasoned politicians, now his allies, provided an odd sense of comfort.

"How will the people of India accept someone like me, with no experience in politics?" he asked, his voice tinged with a mix of incredulity and worry. "There are Muslim citizens who have been awaiting partition, dreaming of a new land. And now, I am to be the one to dash those dreams?" The room fell into a heavy silence, the intensity of his words hanging in the air. It was Ali Bhai who broke the quiet, his voice steady and assuring. "Cyrus," he began, "the memorandum that we have here, bearing the signatures of every member from both the Indian National Party and the Muslim Quam, is a testament to the democratic process we have upheld in this decision. This is not a unilateral appointment; it's a collective consensus, a reflection of the unity and understanding between our parties."

He paused, letting his words sink in, then continued, "The Muslim community, along with the rest of India, will see that they are not being governed by a leader from the majority community. This very fact will ease many of the concerns and apprehensions about bias and favouritism. You represent a neutral choice, an unbiased mediator in a time of great division." Ali Bhai gestured towards the stack of papers on the table. "This signed memorandum will not remain confined to the walls of this room. We intend to circulate it and ensure it's published by every major newspaper across the country. The people will see that this decision has the backing of their elected representatives, that it was reached through careful deliberation and mutual agreement."

Cyrus listened, his mind processing Ali Bhai's words. The responsibility he was about to undertake was colossal, and the path ahead fraught with challenges. Yet, in that moment, he also realized the unprecedented opportunity he had been given to bridge divides and to be the leader of a nation yearning for unity and peace. The governor general's office doors opened with a soft creak, momentarily pulling the attention away from the intense deliberations. Framed against the majestic entrance was Richelle, Cyrus's wife, her elegant figure cast in shadow against the soft glow of the morning sun. Her deep blue dress contrasted sharply with the traditional Indian attire of most who were present in the room.

Cyrus's eyes widened as he saw her. He hadn't expected her to be there, at least not this early, not during this crucial moment.

"Richelle?" Cyrus started, his voice laced with surprise.

Richelle's eyes were wide with disbelief, her voice a tremulous whisper as she clutched the fabric of her dress, still trying to process the whirlwind of events that had unfolded. The morning had started like any other, but in mere hours, their world had turned upside down. The sudden intrusion of the army into their tranquil home had shaken her to the core. Her gaze was fixed on Cyrus, searching for answers, for some semblance of understanding in this chaos. She walked swiftly towards him, her heels clicking against the polished marble floor.

Every eye in the room turned to watch the exchange, their discussions temporarily forgotten.

"Cyrus, what is happening?" she asked, her voice barely audible over the pounding of her heart. "Why did they come for you? Why like this?" The confusion was etched on her face, her brows furrowed in a mix of fear and incredulity.

Cyrus, still grappling with his own shock, took a deep breath, trying to muster some semblance of calm to ease her distress. "Richelle, I..." he admitted, his voice steady but his eyes betraying his turmoil. "This is as unexpected for me as it is for you."

She shivered, the memory of the soldiers storming in still fresh and vivid. "They just barged in, Cyrus. They had guns. I was so scared." Rachel's voice cracked, the terror of the moment gripping her. "I thought... I thought something terrible had happened."

Cyrus sighed, taking her hand and giving it a gentle squeeze. "I'm sorry, Richelle. It's all happened so suddenly. I wanted to tell you, but—"

"But what, Cyrus?" Richelle's voice was sharp, a rare edge of impatience cutting through.

Ali Bhai stepped forward, attempting to ease the tension. "Mrs. Engineer, I understand your concerns. Things have indeed been moving rapidly.

India stands at a historical juncture, and your husband is at the heart of it."

Richelle looked at Ali Bhai, then back to Cyrus, her eyes demanding a clearer explanation.

Panditji cleared his throat. "Richelle, Cyrus has been chosen by the leadership of the major parties to become the next prime minister of India."

Richelle stared, her gaze flitting between the faces in the room, trying to discern if this was some elaborate jest. But the sombre expressions around her confirmed the gravity of the situation.

Taking a deep breath, she replied, "I just… I need a moment." She turned her gaze back to Cyrus, her eyes softening. "We'll talk about this later."

Cyrus nodded, holding her hand tighter for a fleeting moment. "I promise."

As guards escorted Richelle out of the hall, Ali Bhai introduced another figure, a regal man with sharp features and a deep gaze. "Allow me to introduce Shaukat Ali Khan," Ali Bhai declared, his voice ringing with a mix of respect and warmth. "He has been a close confidante and a crucial pillar in many of my endeavours."

Everyone's attention turned to Shaukat. There was an aura of mystery around him, making it clear that there was much more to him than met the eye.

With a courteous nod, Shaukat stepped forward, extending his hand for introductions. The significance of the moment wasn't lost on anyone — they were not merely shaking hands with an ally of Ali Bhai but potentially with someone who could reshape the course of their newly emerging nation.

As the evening progressed, the hallways of the mansion echoed with quiet discussions and whispered plans. It was in one of these quieter corridors that Shaukat beckoned Cyrus with a soft gesture, away from the prying eyes and attentive ears.

Cyrus followed Shaukat's lead and entered a smaller room, faintly lit, exuding an aura of privacy. A young man stood there, his posture upright but with an easy grace. He bore a striking resemblance to Shaukat, with the same deep-set eyes, but there was a spark of youth and fire in them, hinting at dreams yet to be realized and battles yet to be fought.

"My son, Hamid," Shaukat said, pride evident in his voice. "He's recently returned from his studies abroad and has expressed a keen interest in the affairs of our nation. He will be your interim finance minister. His expertise in the global financial landscape is unparalleled."

Cyrus and Hamid exchanged cordial nods, but it was evident that the unexpected promotion sat heavy on them both.

In the aftermath of the unsettling events, Cyrus found himself navigating the corridors like a lost traveller. The small room, once a sanctuary of sorts, now felt like a cage he had just stepped out of. His footsteps were silent, almost ghost-like, as he made his way towards the living room. Each step seemed mechanical, guided more by habit than intention.

He was lost in a sea of thoughts, each one crashing over him with the thought of the uncertainty that now clouded his future. There was a numbness that had settled over him, a quietness that was not peaceful but heavy with unspoken fears and unformed questions.

He stopped midway, his gaze vacant as he stared at nothing in particular. His mind was a tumultuous whirlwind, yet he stood eerily still. The magnitude of the events that had unfolded bore heavily upon him, making each moment feel surreal, as if he were adrift in a dream he couldn't wake up from. As Cyrus regained his bearings, he slowly made his way towards the grand room where the future of his country, and indeed his own, was being decided. The room, usually a space of warmth and hospitality, now felt like a stage for a play he never auditioned for. He could sense the scale of the moment even before he entered.

As Cyrus slowly made his way back to the grand room, a profound sense of destiny enveloped him.

Waiting for him there were Panditji, Patel Sahib, Ali Bhai and Lord Williamson, figures who were not just individuals, but embodiments of ideologies, histories, and aspirations.

Their faces turned towards him as he entered, each pair of eyes holding different expectations.

The sprawling chambers of the governor general's house held stories of centuries, the walls echoing the whispers of the past. Amidst the intricate tapestries and grand chandeliers, Cyrus found himself in the most opulent room, seemingly larger than life yet stifling in its aura.

His appointment as the prime minister of India was an announcement that echoed louder than the grand clock that hung in the hall. Every tick-tock was a reminder of the sands of time slipping away, with expectations growing.

He took a deep breath, the heavy scent of aged wood and polish filling his lungs. "I... I need a moment alone, please," he murmured, his voice barely rising above his emotional burden.

The attendees left, footsteps fading, leaving him alone with his thoughts. The beautiful paintings around seemed to stare, their eyes filled with the weight of history. Cyrus's heart raced. Thoughts of Richelle—their shared dreams, their laughter, and their envisioned future—all stood at a crossroads now.

A tear threatened to spill, his vision blurring as memories of his father enveloped him. The tales of the Zoroastrians, how they found refuge in India, and the ancestral promise of reciprocation played vividly. "If the time ever comes," his father's voice echoed, "repay this land with our actions."

Lost in the maze of his emotions, the rustling of curtains snapped him back.

A mixture of confusion, apprehension, and determination filled Cyrus. The path was undeniably tough, but he wasn't to tread it alone.

With a newfound determination, he straightened his posture and cleared his throat, signalling the staff outside the room. The massive doors swung open, and Ali Bhai, Patel Sahib, and Panditji re-entered, their expressions reflecting a mixture of concern, hope, and anticipation.

Taking a deep breath, Cyrus began, "I have given it deep thought. But for the unity and future of our great nation, I'm willing to serve as the interim prime minister until fresh elections can be held." He paused, letting the significance of his words hang in the air.

Panditji nodded with approval, his face showing a mixture of relief and admiration. "Your decision shows your love and commitment to this country, Cyrus. I assure you, you will have our unwavering support."

Patel Sahib offered a small smile. "It's a wise decision. India needs a firm hand and a steady heart. The challenges ahead are many, but together, we can overcome them."

Ali Bhai, his ever-observant eyes scanning Cyrus, stepped forward. "Cyrus, remember, every journey starts with a single step. Your choice today is that step for our country."

Taking a moment to gather his emotions, Cyrus continued, "However, I must make one thing clear: This will be an interim arrangement. I shall lead, I shall guide, but when the nation is stable, and when it's time for fresh elections, I expect and insist on a smooth transition."

The room, brimming with the remnants of past choices and the hope of a fresh start, echoed with silent agreement.

Panditji, noticing a lull in the conversation, took the opportunity to introduce another essential player in the unfolding saga of independent India.

"Cyrus," Panditji began, with a slight grin playing on his lips, "allow me to introduce Mr. Nair. Your special secretary."

From the corner of the room emerged a diminutive figure, barely reaching Panditji's shoulders. Mr. Nair had deep-set eyes that twinkled mischievously beneath a pair of thick, black-rimmed glasses, making him appear both scholarly and a tad comical. His neatly combed hair was prematurely greying at the temples, perhaps the price paid for his sharp wit and wisdom. He wore a pristine white cotton shirt, tucked neatly into a pair of black trousers held up by suspenders. The ensemble was completed with traditional brown sandals (paaduka style), simplistic in design yet steeped in cultural significance, making it evident that he was a proud South Indian at heart.

But it was not just his attire that caught Cyrus's attention. It was the aura of the man. Despite his unimposing stature, Mr. Nair carried himself with an air of confidence and had a spring in his step. His wide grin and friendly demeanour immediately put people at ease, and there was an infectious energy about him that drew others in.

As Mr. Nair stepped forward, extending his hand, his voice, surprisingly deep for such a small frame, boomed through the room. "Ah, Prime Minister! It's an absolute pleasure. And don't worry, I'm not as serious as my title suggests." He winked, causing Panditji and a few others in the room to chuckle.

Cyrus, shaking his hand, thought, *This journey is going to be anything but dull with Mr. Nair around.*

August 15, 1947: 2:30 p.m.

As the last strains of the national anthem faded away, reverberating applause echoed throughout the vast grounds. Cyrus, having just taken his oath as the new prime minister, felt the load of an entire nation on his shoulders.

His entourage of guards formed a protective shield around him, guiding him through the swell of the crowd towards the sprawling edifice that was once the viceroy's residence. As he walked, familiar faces from the freedom struggle, political allies, and members of the press flashed by.

Patel Sahib, Panditji, and Ali Bhai trailed behind, whispering among themselves, plans and strategies already being formulated for the challenges ahead. Their intense discussions were momentarily halted when Cyrus paused and turned towards them.

"I appreciate everyone's enthusiasm, but I must admit, today's events have been rather overwhelming," he admitted, taking off his spectacles and rubbing the bridge of his nose. "I need a moment to process, to breathe. I'd like to spend some time with Richelle."

Before anyone could respond, Lord Williamson interjected. "Prime Minister," he began, his voice authoritative, "the viceroy's residence has been repurposed for your use. We've already moved

Mrs. Richelle to the new prime minister's residence. Everything is in order for you both."

Cyrus paused, absorbing the information. "Thank you, Governor General. In that case, I'd like to call it a day." He turned to address the collective. "There's a long journey ahead, and I need to be at my best. Let's regroup and hit the ground running tomorrow."

There were murmurs of understanding and agreement. As Cyrus began moving again, Patel Sahib caught up with him, placing a reassuring hand on his shoulder. "Take all the time you need," he whispered.

Lord Williamson led Cyrus towards a gleaming black car waiting at the foot of the steps. As the vehicle roared to life and began to move, Cyrus looked out of the window, the vast, manicured lawns of the residence stretching out before him. A new chapter was beginning, and he hoped he was ready for whatever lay ahead.

August 15, 1947: The Prime Minister's Residence, Three Hours after Oath-Taking

Later that evening, in the confines of their temporary residence in Delhi, Richelle confronted Cyrus. Inside the Engineer residence, the room was thick with tension. Tears streaming down, she exclaimed,

"How can you agree to this madness? We had plans, Cyrus. A life away from this!"

Cyrus gently took her hands. "Richelle, I didn't ask for this. But if my appointment can prevent the division of my homeland, prevent potential bloodshed… how can I turn away?"

Richelle, her voice choked with emotion, replied, "But at what cost? Your life? Our future?"

Cyrus, still grappling with the encumbrance of his latest responsibility, tried to rationalize the situation. "Richelle," he began, his voice steady, "our ancestors witnessed this land conquered and reshaped over centuries. The least I can do is to try and ensure that it remains united in its most crucial hour."

Richelle paced, her fingers nervously playing with the locket around her neck, a gift from her grandmother. "Cyrus, it's not just the politics. It's the tremendous pressure, the danger, the myriad challenges that this nation will face. Are you truly ready for this?"

He stood up, gazing out at the vast expanse of the city. "Am I ready? I don't know. But I believe in serendipity, and perhaps there's a reason I'm here in this moment."

August 16, 1947:
The Prime Minister's Office

As the first light of dawn streaked across the sky, the city of Delhi was gradually waking up. There was an air of anticipation, of hope mixed with uncertainty. The euphoria of Independence Day was still palpable, but the challenges of a newborn nation were also beginning to set in.

Inside a stately room at the heart of the city, an antique table stood laden with files, maps, and a carafe of freshly brewed tea. The soft chirping of birds and the distant sounds of a city waking up filled the room.

Cyrus sat at the head of the table, his eyes slightly weary but determined. On his left was Panditji while to his right was Patel Sahib.

Adjacent to them were Ali Bhai, = and his confidante Hamid. Both brought with them not just the essence of the Muslim Quam but also the hope of seamless integration in this new India.

Nair, efficient as ever, stood a little away, his notebook in hand, ready to jot down decisions, actions, and notes. His presence, often understated, was the backbone of many such high-powered discussions.

The mood was intense. The import of the decisions to be made was evident. The unity of a diverse nation, the intricacies of governance, and the looming shadows of partition—everything was at stake.

Cyrus, clearing his throat, initiated the discussion. "Gentlemen, the path ahead is challenging. We have immense responsibilities, and the world watches us closely. We must ensure our decisions reflect the aspirations of every Indian."

Panditji spread out several parchments on the table, marking territories, regions, and districts. "Before we delve into governance, there's the matter of territory integration. Without partition, this nation will be vast, both geographically and culturally. We need a vision."

Ali Bhai joined in, his demeanour composed. "The Muslim Quam trusts in this united vision. But our people need assurance. Assurance that they will have equal rights and a voice."

Cyrus nodded. "We must frame a constitution that speaks to every Indian. It must echo the principles of unity, equality, and fraternity."

Panditji, looking pleased, added, "And until that constitution is formed, you will have the advisory committee's complete support. Remember, you were chosen not just for political reasons but for the legacy of fairness and justice your family upholds."

The discussions went deep into the night, touching upon subjects like the economy, infrastructure, defence, and international relations. Hamid Khan, with his financial acumen, highlighted the need for a stable economy. "Trade, commerce, international alliances—we'll have to rethink everything from scratch."

Cyrus, despite the enormity of the tasks ahead, felt a glimmer of hope. Surrounded by some of the best minds, he believed they could indeed create a nation that future generations would be proud of.

A soft voice interrupted his thoughts. It was Patel Sahib. "You seem troubled, Mr. Engineer."

Cyrus looked up, slightly surprised. "It's just the burden of this responsibility. It feels like walking on a tightrope."

Patel Sahib smiled, "It is. But remember, the winds might try to topple you, but your core, your intent, will keep you balanced. My father always believed in coexistence. We may have different paths, but our destination is the same. Unity."

Cyrus nodded. "I appreciate the support. Together, I believe we can make this vision a reality."

There were challenges aplenty. From border disputes to economic policies, from cultural integration to ensuring religious harmony, the road to forming a united India was filled with obstacles. But Cyrus, with the unwavering support of his advisory committee, continued to tread the path with determination.

The day was a whirlwind, one that would define the course of the nation for the coming decades. The clock seemed to be racing against them, ticking away relentlessly. The hours were packed with back-to-back meetings. Delegates from various regions, representatives from minority groups, and leaders of significant communities all waited their turn to present their concerns and aspirations to the newly appointed leader.

Each meeting was its own universe of concerns. There were also economic worries, with the treasury nearly empty.

In one room, scholars debated the principles that would underpin the new constitution. In another, economists discussed potential trade routes and rebuilding the economy post the British exit. There were diplomats negotiating treaties, civil servants drafting policies, and military strategists planning the defence of the borders.

Throughout it all, Cyrus was the centre, the eye of the storm. He listened, intervened, decided, and reassured. With every decision he made, with every assurance he gave, the burden on his shoulders grew heavier.

By the time the evening shadows began to creep in, the corridors, once bustling with activity, had started to empty. The aroma of evening chai wafted through, signalling the close of an exhaustive day.

Dragging his weary body and an even wearier mind, Cyrus finally made his way to his temporary residence. The residence, though less grand than the governor general's mansion, had an air of tranquillity, a peaceful oasis amidst the chaos of the capital.

As he stepped in, the familiar aroma of his favourite Parsi dish filled the air. And there, in the centre of the living room, stood Richelle, his anchor in these stormy times. Her warm smile provided the comfort he so desperately sought. Without a word, they embraced, finding solace in each other's presence.

As they sat down for dinner, the enormity of the day's events, the monumental decisions made, and the challenges yet to come all seemed a bit more bearable with her by his side.

Richelle, feeling increasingly isolated and concerned, finally confronted him. "Cyrus, every hour I fear for you. I see the stress, the threats, and the politics. I miss our life in Bombay, our dreams of a quiet future in England."

Cyrus took her in his arms. "Richelle, this journey won't be forever. Once the foundation is laid, once India finds its footing, we'll revisit our dreams. For now, I need you by my side, more than ever."

The emotional toll, the political machinations, the hopes of a nation—Cyrus Engineer was in the eye of the storm. But as history has shown, it's in the most challenging moments that true leaders emerge. And as the days passed, India started to see the dawn of a new era, united and resilient under its unexpected leader.

Chapter 2

THE RIPPLES OF DESTINY

August 17, 1947: New Delhi

As Cyrus entered the Prime Minister's Office, a space still unfamiliar and imposing, his eyes were immediately drawn to the array of newspapers spread across the desk. The headlines screamed out, each offering a different perspective on his sudden ascent to the country's leadership.

One headline caught his eye, bold and somewhat flattering: 'Cyrus: The Unsung Hero Who Saved Partition'. The article beneath it painted him as a saviour, a man whose unexpected rise to power had single-handedly prevented the division of a nation. For a moment, Cyrus allowed himself a faint smile. The notion of being seen as a hero was both gratifying and overwhelming.

But as his gaze shifted, another headline starkly contrasted the first: 'Inexperienced Cyrus at the Helm: Was Partition a Better Option?' This piece was openly critical, questioning his ability to govern a nation as complex and divided as India. It spoke of his lack of political experience, painting a picture of a novice who had found himself in the country's highest office more by chance than by qualification.

While political negotiations and power transitions continued behind closed doors, the streets outside resonated with the voices of those who felt left out, overlooked, or vehemently opposed to certain decisions.

A particular faction, the Rashtriya Swayamsevak Dal (RSD), voiced their concerns vehemently. The RSD, deeply rooted in the cause of a Hindu-majoritarian nation, had their reservations about the newly appointed prime minister. But it wasn't his Parsi background they had an issue with. It was the presence of his British-born wife, Richelle, that stirred the pot.

The intensity of the situation escalated when news reached the PM's residence that a protest was planned in front of the gates the next day. An atmosphere of unease blanketed the corridors of power. Officials scurried about, strategizing on how to handle the situation without causing an uproar.

Cyrus sat in his sprawling office, staring at the evening sun.

He was interrupted by a soft knock. It was Richelle. With the events of the last few hours, he had hardly gotten a moment with her. She looked sombre, her usually bright eyes clouded with worry. She softly said, "Cyrus, I overheard the staff discussing the planned protest. Maybe… maybe I should leave for London. At least for a while. If my presence is a thorn in the side of the people—"

Cyrus interrupted, "No. Running away is not the solution. I chose you, and I chose India. Both choices I made with full consciousness and pride. You're a part of this journey, just as much as I am."

She smiled faintly, taking solace in his words, but the fear lingered. "I just don't want to be the reason for unrest or your unpopularity. We dreamt of a peaceful life, and look where we've landed."

Patel Sahib, overhearing the conversation as he walked past the office, decided to weigh in. "Richelle," he began in his baritone voice, "your nationality or ancestry should not dictate how people perceive Cyrus's leadership. It's an excuse, a front for deeper divides and concerns. But remember, these are the teething troubles of a young, free nation. Give it time."

The conversation was interrupted by an urgent message. A delegation from the RSD was seeking an audience with the prime minister. Cyrus decided to face the situation head-on. "Give them an appointment first thing tomorrow morning," he declared.

As the rays of the morning sun warmed the elegant living room of the prime minister's residence on August 18, Cyrus found himself preparing for a meeting he'd been anticipating with a mix of curiosity and concern. He was to meet with the secretary of the RSD, Mr. Bhosle.

Mr. Bhosle made a pronounced entrance. Despite his short stature, his heavy build and formidable demeanour commanded attention. His traditional Maratha turban sat atop his head, making him look slightly taller, and his dark eyes scanned the room methodically before settling on Cyrus.

"Mr. Prime Minister," Bhosle greeted with a nod, the formal tone barely concealing the underlying tension.

"Mr. Bhosle," Cyrus replied courteously. "Thank you for coming. Please, have a seat."

Bhosle's gaze lingered for a moment before he spoke, "I'll get straight to the point, Mr. Cyrus. The nation's helm is a significant responsibility. While I respect your dedication, there are concerns in my organization about the… origins of your spouse. India's prime minister's wife being of non-Indian origin is… unsettling."

Before Cyrus could respond, Patel Sahib, who had been silently observing, intervened. "Mr. Bhosle, your apprehensions are noted. But let me assure you, a person's marital choices don't dictate their national allegiance or the sincerity of their service. I've known Cyrus long enough to vouch for his unwavering commitment to India."

Cyrus nodded, grateful for Patel Sahib's support. "Mr. Bhosle, India's identity is rooted in its diverse, inclusive ethos. Let's not lose sight of that," he added.

Bhosle's face remained stern. "India's identity is at stake," he responded. "We must be vigilant about the influences we allow. You should understand, Mr. Cyrus, my concerns stem not from personal prejudice but from a deeply ingrained fear of foreign intervention. Our history is riddled with invasions and influence from outsiders. Can you blame us for being wary?"

Cyrus leaned forward, clasping his hands together. "Mr. Bhosle, I appreciate your candidness, and I understand the historical context that fuels such concerns. But let me reiterate—India's strength lies in her diversity and inclusivity. Every decision I make is, and will be, in the best interest of our nation. And as for Richelle, her nationality doesn't determine her commitment to India or mine."

A momentary silence engulfed the room, only to be broken by Nair, who entered bearing a tray of steaming chai and snacks. As he set it down, the aroma of fresh ginger tea wafted through, subtly cutting the tension in the room.

Panditji chimed in gently, "We've gained our freedom after much sacrifice, Mr. Bhosle. The last thing we'd want is to be bound by prejudices and doubts. Let us look ahead, focus on uniting our people and rebuilding our nation. This is a time for collaboration, not confrontation."

Bhosle's stern face exhibited a flicker of contemplation. "I stand by my concerns," he said, "but I will also respect the office of the prime minister. Let us hope your tenure proves my apprehensions wrong."

While no immediate resolutions were reached, the meeting set the tone for Cyrus's tenure. It would be a path laden with challenges, both personal and political.

August 20, 1947

The atmosphere in the prime minister's residence was heavy with debates, decisions, and discussions.

Outside the walls, however, a different story was unfolding. The serene ambience of the residence was disrupted as Nair hurriedly entered, clutching a folded newspaper. "Sir, you must see this," he said, handing the paper to Cyrus.

The headline screamed, "Massive Rally at Ram Leela Maidan to Protest PM Appointment!" The article detailed how a prominent leader of the RSD,

Suresh Mansekar, had galvanized thousands to voice their opposition to Cyrus's role as the prime minister. The accompanying photograph showed a sea of people, placards in hand, fervour in their eyes.

Panditji sighed. "It was only a matter of time. The nation is in flux, and such opposition is expected."

As dusk approached, the heart of Delhi, Ram Leela Maidan, pulsed with intensity. Amidst the cacophony of shouted slogans, Suresh, a tall figure with a piercing gaze and a commanding presence, stood on the makeshift dais. "This is our Bharat, the land of our ancestors! How can we let someone, especially with ties to a foreigner, lead us?" he thundered, drawing roars of agreement from the crowd.

"Our motherland," he began, his voice echoing amidst a sea of saffron flags, "has just emerged from the dark shadows of the British Raj. We've suffered, bled, and sacrificed to reclaim Bharat. And yet, today, we stand at the risk of letting another British mark taint the highest office of our land."

He continued, "Cyrus's capabilities as a leader may not be in question, but the symbolism of his union with a British woman cannot be ignored. How can we accept another reminder of our colonial past in the prime minister's residence? We've fought too hard to erase the British influence, and we will not let it seep back in!"

The crowd responded with roaring applause and chants, "Bharat for Bharatiyas! No more British influence!"

Back at the residence, Cyrus, Patel Sahib, and the others convened in the central room, pondering their next move. "We must address this," Cyrus declared. "Ignoring such a significant public sentiment is not an option."

Patel Sahib nodded. "We'll need to engage directly, perhaps even organize a counter-rally or an open dialogue. At the very least, a public address might be in order."

Amidst this turbulent atmosphere, whispered conversations in the tea stalls and markets questioned the wisdom of placing Cyrus at the helm. They debated, "Does his marriage to Richelle make him more sympathetic to the British? Will he always be under the influence of the West?"

August 25, 1947:
The Prime Minister's Residence

Cyrus was seated at the head of the long teakwood table, a sense of determination and responsibility evident in his demeanour. As the representatives presented their cases, he listened attentively, occasionally scribbling notes. Panditji was to his right, whispering insights while Mr. Nair lightened the tense atmosphere with sporadic goofy humour.

Suddenly, a frantic knock sounded at the door. Everyone in the room turned to see an out-of-breath junior aide rush in. His eyes darted across the room before settling on the prime minister. "Sir," he panted, "urgent news!"

Cyrus's eyes met the aide's. "What is it?" he asked, sensing the urgency in the aide's tone.

"An earthquake, sir," the aide replied, his voice trembling. "It's struck Bombay. Preliminary reports suggest it's massive."

A heavy silence descended upon the room. The clamour of discussions, arguments, and deliberations was instantly replaced by a vacuum of disbelief. Every face turned ashen, reflecting the shock of the moment. The very fabric of the nation seemed to quake.

Panditji stood up, his usually composed face etched with concern. "Details," he demanded.

"We're still gathering information," the aide replied. "But it's catastrophic. The epicentre was close to the city."

Mr. Nair now looked grave. "We need to act immediately," he said.

Cyrus, absorbing the news, took a deep breath. Pushing aside the prepared agenda, he declared, "The priorities have shifted. We must mobilize relief operations immediately. Every second counts."

The room, initially paralyzed by shock, sprang into action. The leaders, realizing the gravity of the situation, set aside their differences, uniting in their commitment to aid the stricken city.

Ministers and advisors scrambled to their feet, trying to get through to their districts, their families. The old walls of the room seemed to reverberate with the collective anxiety. Panditji clutched at his turban, murmuring prayers under his breath. Ali Bhai's hand shook as he dialled number after number on the rotary phone, desperate for a connection.

Without missing a beat, Cyrus turned to Mr. Nair. "I need to be in Bombay. Arrange a flight at the earliest," he ordered.

Nair nodded briskly. "Right away, Mr. Prime Minister."

Within hours, Cyrus was aboard a plane, flying over the vast expanse of the country, making his way to the heart of the devastation. As the plane began its descent into Bombay, he peered out of the window. The first glimpses of the city were harrowing.

Historic edifices that once stood tall, symbols of Bombay's architectural grandeur, were now crumbling ruins. Dust clouds enveloped entire streets, and from his aerial vantage point, Cyrus could make out the chaotic movement of people, like ants in distress. The once bustling streets were filled with debris, shattered glass, and the remnants of structures that had succumbed to the force of nature.

The iconic Gateway of India, which had always stood as a proud testament to India's colonial past and its resilient spirit, now looked vulnerable, with visible cracks running up its façade. Nearby, the majestic Taj Mahal Palace Hotel, a symbol of Bombay's affluence and elegance, had portions of its roof caved in.

Cyrus's heart ached at the sight. Bombay, the city of dreams, was experiencing its worst nightmare. He felt a deep responsibility; he was not just the leader of the nation but its beacon of hope during these trying times. The gravity of the situation weighed heavily on him, but he knew he had to stay strong for his people.

As the plane touched down, a convoy awaited him.

The earthquake's wrath had left its mark on Cyrus's palatial mansion as well. While the structure stood resilient, the opulence within bore witness to nature's fury. Cracks snaked along the walls like intricate, unwanted artwork. A once-immaculate chandelier now hung askew, its crystals trembling with each aftershock. Porcelain vases lay shattered, their fragments scattered across the marble floor like petals after a storm. Books had tumbled from shelves, creating a chaotic landscape in the once orderly library. It was damage that, while not compromising the mansion's grandeur, was enough to remind everyone of nature's unpredictable power.

As Cyrus surveyed the damage wrought by the earthquake, Mr. Nair stepped forward, his expression a blend of concern and resolve. "Sir, considering the state of the mansion, it's not safe for you to stay here," he said, eyeing the cracks in the walls and the debris scattered around.

Cyrus nodded solemnly, the gravity of the situation evident in his gaze. He understood the need for caution, even though the thought of leaving his home, even temporarily, felt unsettling.

"Where will I go, Nair?" Cyrus asked, his voice tinged with weariness.

"I've arranged for you to stay in a government guest house. It's about fifty kilometres from Bombay, far from the quake's impact zone. It's a safe distance, and the house is well-appointed and comfortable," Nair explained, his tone reassuring.

Cyrus paused for a moment, taking in the information. The thought of being so far from the city, from the centre of his responsibilities, was daunting. Yet, he knew the importance of safety, not just for himself but for the continuity of governance.

"Is it secure?" Cyrus inquired, his mind already shifting to the practicalities.

"Absolutely, sir. It's one of the most secure locations we have. It's a fancy place, quite secluded and peaceful. You'll have everything you need there," Nair assured him.

Cyrus finally nodded, accepting the situation. "All right, let's make arrangements to move. I trust your judgment, Nair."

With a sense of urgency, Nair coordinated the move. Soon, Cyrus found himself in a car, driving away from the damaged grandeur of his mansion, towards a temporary abode that promised safety and a chance to regroup amidst the chaos left by nature's unforeseen ferocity.

In the midst of this chaos emerged stories of both heartbreak and heroism. A mother, trapped under the debris of her home, managed to shield her infant, sacrificing her life so that her child might live. A group of teenagers, who had been practising for a local cricket match, suddenly found themselves lifting heavy beams and bricks, rescuing those pinned underneath. Everywhere you looked, ordinary people were stepping up, showcasing extraordinary courage.

But amid the tales of bravery, there were also stories of staggering loss. An entire school, with over a hundred children, was flattened in mere seconds. A young groom, who had been preparing for his wedding that very evening, was found lifeless, still clutching the wedding ring he was to give his bride.

As the sun set on that fateful day, the streets that were once filled with cries of despair slowly began to echo with songs of hope. Campfires sprouted across the city, around which families and strangers huddled together, sharing food and stories and lending each other strength. Cyrus, abandoning the confines of the government guest house, decided to walk amidst his people. Flanked by a few guards, he wandered through the devastated streets. He lent a hand where he could, lifting beams, offering comfort, and listening to the heartbreaking stories of those who had lost everything.

At one campfire, he met an elderly woman named Devika. Her hands, wrinkled and scarred from a lifetime of labour, cradled a small, dusty photo frame. It was an old black-and-white picture of her family, all of whom she'd lost to the earthquake.

"My boy," she began, her voice trembling, "I've lived a long life. I've seen the birth of this nation and dreamt of its future. And in all these years, I've never witnessed such unity." Her eyes filled with tears as she continued, "Today, I saw a Sikh man helping a Muslim child, a Hindu woman comforting a Christian mother. In our darkest hour, the true spirit of India has shone the brightest."

Moved by her words, Cyrus knelt beside her, taking her hand in his. "Your strength and wisdom embody the very spirit of this nation. And it's on this foundation of unity and resilience that we will rebuild, stronger and united."

Word of Cyrus's on-the-ground efforts spread like wildfire. The people, once uncertain of this Parsi leader with a British wife, began to see him as one of their own. He wasn't just a leader giving orders from above; he was a fellow countryman, grieving, toiling, and rebuilding alongside them.

RSD, despite its concerns regarding Richelle's nationality, couldn't ignore Cyrus's genuine efforts. While they maintained their reservations, there was a growing respect for the man who was leading the country through its worst crisis.

The days that followed saw relief pouring in from every corner of the country and beyond. Trucks laden with food, water, and medical supplies made their way to the affected regions. Volunteers from all over the country descended on the city, helping in the herculean task of rebuilding.

Shortly after Cyrus's hasty departure to Bombay, he summoned the key stakeholders to the city, intent on overseeing the relief efforts personally. Panditji, Patel Sahib, and Ali Bhai, understanding the gravity of the situation, quickly followed suit. Their journey to Bombay was not just a response to the call of duty but a testament to the unified front the leadership needed to present in times of national calamity.

As the magnitude of the earthquake's destruction unfurled before them, the country's leaders gathered in an emergency meeting at a makeshift centre—one of the few structures that seemed to have partly withstood the catastrophe.

While the epicentre was busy grappling with the aftermath of the earthquake, inside the PM's makeshift centre, a gravity-defying paperweight rolled off Cyrus's desk. Mr. Nair, walking in, commented, "I guess even the paperweights are trying to escape duties, eh, Mr. Prime Minister?"

Cyrus, appreciating the momentary distraction, smiled and replied, "It seems so, Nair."

As the dust settled, amidst the chaos, emerged a figure who would later become an instrumental pillar in the world of media and politics— Mrs. Chatterjee.

Panditji, amidst the tumult, was coordinating rescue efforts when Patel Sahib walked over to him, holding the arm of a young woman with sharp eyes that mirrored her determination. "Panditji," Patel

Sahib began, "this is Mrs. Chatterjee. She's been leading the communication efforts here, keeping the public informed and calm despite the devastation. The way she's handling this crisis, I believe she has the potential to be the media advisor to the prime minister."

Mrs. Chatterjee, always stern in demeanour, nodded in acknowledgement. Her saree was covered in dust, and her hair had come loose, but her spirit remained indomitable. She spoke, her voice a mix of authority and compassion, "We need to ensure that accurate information gets out to the public, preventing rumours and panic. Also, the nation should see the gravity of the situation, pushing them to unite and help."

Panditji was impressed. "In times of crisis, true leaders emerge. Mrs. Chatterjee, once we get through this, I would be honoured if you'd consider Patel Sahib's suggestion."

The air was thick, not just with the dust and debris from the aftermath but also with tension. Reports of shortages in food, water, and medical supplies, coupled with the rising death toll, lay heavily upon them.

Patel Sahib broke the silence. "The devastation is beyond our immediate capacity. We need all hands on deck."

He paused, taking a moment to gauge the reactions in the room. "And that includes the RSD. Say what you will about them, but they have the largest volunteer base ready to mobilize. We need that manpower."

Ali Bhai, an eloquent speaker known for his command over Urdu and Hindi, immediately retorted, "Patel Sahib, are you suggesting we collaborate with a group that has shown blatant resistance to Cyrus's leadership? Their ideology doesn't align with our vision for a united India."

Hamid, younger than Ali Bhai but just as fierce, chimed in, "They won't serve without an agenda. Their assistance will come at a cost. And that might be the very soul of our nation."

Cyrus, absorbing the heated arguments around him, finally raised his hand for silence. "I appreciate everyone's concerns. But our priority now is our people. Every minute we waste here is costing lives out there. We can settle our ideological differences later."

Patel Sahib, seizing the moment, pressed on, "The RSD has a disciplined cadre. They're organized, efficient, and right now, we desperately need that."

Cyrus, deep in thought, finally spoke. "I believe I may have a solution." All eyes turned to him. "Gokhale and Patel Sahib have shared some respectful conversations in the past. While they might not see eye to eye on all fronts, I believe in his commitment to the country."

Ali Bhai, sceptical but willing to listen, responded, "So, you suggest we reach out to Gokhale?"

"Yes," Cyrus said firmly. "He might be our bridge to the RSD. If we can channel their discipline and manpower for relief efforts, it could be a significant step towards healing—both for the victims of the earthquake and the divides within our country."

With a heavy heart and the mantle of leadership on his shoulders, Cyrus approached Gokhale later that evening. The two men, representing different facets of the country, sat across from each other.

Mr. Gokhale, the president of RSD, was a man of impressive stature, tall with a well-built physique. His deep-set eyes always held a penetrating gaze, looking as though they had seen many battles and emerged victorious from them all. His salt-and-pepper beard, neatly trimmed, added to his aura of wisdom and experience.

Dressed invariably in the traditional khaki shorts and white shirt, the uniform of the RSD, he was a staunch nationalist and a proud Hindu. Gokhale had an unwavering belief in the Hindu way of life, regarding it as a guide to moral and societal well-being. His life was dedicated to upholding and promoting the values of ancient Hindu traditions.

Yet, for all his staunch beliefs, Gokhale wasn't a man of mere rhetoric. His charisma was matched by his pragmatism. He understood that while ideals set the direction, compromise, and collaboration got things done. He was revered by his followers, not just because he upheld Hindu values but because he fought tirelessly for a united and self-reliant India.

Though often at loggerheads with the mainstream political narrative of the time, Gokhale's influence was undeniable. His vast network of RSD cadres was disciplined and could mobilize rapidly, making them an essential force in any national effort.

As the two leaders met, the air was thick with tension and anticipation. Two men, representing different visions for India, but sharing a common love for their motherland, were about to engage in a dialogue that would shape the nation's future.

"India is bleeding, Gokhale," Cyrus began, his voice filled with emotion. "We might have our differences, but I know you care for this nation as deeply as I do."

Gokhale, usually stern, showed a hint of emotion. "These are testing times, Mr. Prime Minister. And you're right. Our ideologies might differ, but our love for this country is unwavering."

"Then let us join hands," Cyrus extended his own, "and let us mobilize the RSD volunteers for the greater good. Together, we can help our nation rise from these ruins."

Gokhale, after what seemed like an eternity, finally shook Cyrus's hand. "For India," he said.

"For India," Cyrus echoed. And with that handshake, a new chapter of collaboration began in the annals of India's history.

Gokhale immediately dispatched thousands of his dal sipahis to the affected areas. They set up makeshift relief camps, providing food, water, and first aid to the injured. Their expertise in crowd management came in handy in managing the large number of distraught citizens, directing them to safer areas and coordinating search and rescue missions.

The cadres were not only the hands and feet on the ground but also brought with them a spirit of selfless service, or 'seva'. Their ethos was rooted in the ancient Hindu philosophy of 'Vasudhaiva Kutumbakam' — the world is one family. In these trying times, they embodied this principle to the fullest.

Many stories of heroism emerged. Young dal sipahis risked their lives to pull people out of the debris while others formed human chains to pass along supplies or to remove rubble. Senior members, leveraging their ties in the community, organized donations and supplies, ensuring the continuous flow of necessities.

Amid the despair, there was a notable incident where a group of RSD cadres formed a protective circle around a mosque during prayer times, ensuring the safety of the Muslim community amidst the chaos. This act went a long way in cementing the organization's role in promoting communal harmony.

Cyrus, witnessing the dedication and fervour of the RSD cadres, couldn't help but admire their spirit. Their rapid response and systematic approach were invaluable in the immediate aftermath of the disaster. The dal sipahis worked hand in hand with the army, police, and other civilian groups, becoming a beacon of hope in the city's darkest hours.

Over time, the immediate rescue operations transitioned into rehabilitation and reconstruction. The RSD played a crucial role in building temporary shelters, sanitizing water sources, and even reconstructing religious sites across different faiths.

Bombay, in all its resilience, started its journey to healing and rebuilding. The harmonious collaboration between the government and various organizations, including the RSD, showcased the indomitable spirit of India. The tragedy had brought to the fore an essential lesson—unity in diversity—and the strength in coming together for a greater cause.

September 2, 1947: New Delhi

Cyrus stood by a window, his silhouette outlined by the soft evening light. As Gokhale entered, he turned, his face, revealing the strains of recent events.

With every topic they discussed, a certain camaraderie developed between Gokhale and Cyrus. It was evident in the way they began referring to each other by their first names, a departure from the formalities that marked the beginning of their conversation.

"You know, Cyrus," Gokhale began, with a hint of amusement, "if anyone had told me I'd be sitting in the prime minister's residence at this hour, discussing the future of India with you, I'd have said they were out of their minds."

Cyrus chuckled. "Life has its way of presenting the most unexpected scenarios, Mr. Gokhale. Just a few weeks ago, I was contemplating a life in London with Richelle. And here I am, grappling with the aftermath of one of the most devastating earthquakes our nation has seen."

Gokhale sipped on his tea, appreciating the brief pause. "You have heavy responsibilities on your shoulders, Cyrus. But it's not just yours to bear. Together, we can make it lighter."

Cyrus replied, "Times of crisis show us who our true allies are. The work of your cadres post the earthquake… it's been exemplary, Gokhale."

Gokhale smirked slightly. "So, this isn't a social call then?"

Cyrus sighed and gestured for him to sit. "I've been considering something. I need someone reliable by my side, especially now, with everything in turmoil. Someone who can handle the Home Ministry with efficiency."

Gokhale, raising an eyebrow, responded, "You're not thinking of me, are you? After all, we've had our differences."

Cyrus nodded. "Yes, we have. But differences can be assets. You have the respect of the masses, Gokhale. And your dedication to the nation is undeniable." Gokhale paused, considering the offer. "This isn't about power, Cyrus. It's about the future of this nation. Do you truly believe I'm the right person for this?"

Cyrus replied earnestly, "I do. The country needs a mix of ideologies to thrive, not just one voice echoing in a chamber."

Gokhale raised an eyebrow, his gaze piercing. "Cyrus, while I'm honoured by your offer, I must ask, do you have the authority to make this decision independently? Shouldn't such appointments be consulted with the advisory committee?"

Cyrus leaned forward, understanding the importance of Gokhale's question. "I appreciate your concern, Mr. Gokhale. But let me assure you, the suggestion to appoint you as home minister came from Patel Sahib himself. He recognized your immense contribution and leadership during the recent earthquake crisis. Your efforts in coordinating the relief work were nothing short of extraordinary."

Gokhale's expression softened slightly, a hint of surprise flickering in his eyes. "Patel Sahib recommended me?" he asked, his tone a mix of disbelief and curiosity.

"Yes, he did," Cyrus affirmed. "And frankly, I saw no reason to disagree. Your expertise and dedication during the earthquake relief operations were exemplary. You showed remarkable leadership and resilience in the face of adversity. Our nation needs someone of your calibre to oversee its internal security and well-being."

"Very well, Cyrus," Gokhale finally said, nodding slowly. "If Patel Sahib believes in my capabilities and you concur, I am willing to accept this responsibility on one condition—that we always prioritize the nation over politics."

Cyrus extended his hand, "Agreed. Welcome aboard, Home Minister Gokhale."

Their handshake sealed the beginning of a new chapter for India.

The atmosphere in the prime minister's residence was thick with anticipation. It was an alliance nobody saw coming, especially given the differences between the two powerful men. Both leaders knew that eyes across the nation were upon them. Their alliance wasn't just symbolic; it was pivotal for the unity and rebuilding of post-earthquake India.

"Tell me, Gokhale," Cyrus began, swirling the amber liquid in his glass, "why did the RSD respond so quickly? Why deploy your cadres for disaster relief?"

Gokhale met Cyrus's eyes. "Because, Cyrus, before being Hindus or Muslims or Christians, we are Indians. Every person suffering in the aftermath of the quake is a brother, a sister. And the Rashtriya Swayamsevak Dal believes in service to the nation first."

A deep silence settled between them. Both leaders had so often been on opposing sides, yet in this dire time, they found themselves needing each other.

Cyrus cleared his throat. "The nation is watching us, Gokhale. Watching to see if we'll falter, if this newfound alliance will crumble."

Gokhale leaned forward. "Then let's show them unity. Let's show them that when push comes to shove, we stand united for India."

The words seemed to hang in the room, their heft pushing away past animosities. It was a pivotal moment. A moment where both leaders understood the importance of coming together for the greater good.

Cyrus finally said, "Your cadres have shown their strength and dedication. But they are not soldiers. We need to ensure their safety as they help rebuild."

Gokhale responded, "The RSD believes in discipline and training. But you are right, they are not soldiers. However, they are committed to the cause of the nation. We've faced many challenges, and this is just another one."

Cyrus nodded. "We need to work closely then. Not just in the cities but in the rural areas, too. The devastation is widespread. Our combined strength can help India rise again."

The evening wore on as the two leaders continued their discussions, laying out plans and strategies. They talked about logistics, manpower, resources, and the mammoth task of rebuilding a city torn apart.

As the clock chimed midnight, Cyrus stood up and stretched. "It's late. But I feel we've made progress. I know this partnership will take time to strengthen, but I'm optimistic."

Gokhale smiled. "Optimism is the first step to success. Here's to a new beginning, Mr. Prime Minister."

September 25, 1947: The Prime Minister's Office

Cyrus sat behind the large desk, his silhouette sharp against the glow of the morning sun. He was engrossed in the myriad files strewn about, the remnants of a nation in flux. Every so often, the soft whisper of pages turning was interrupted by the chirping of birds outside or the distant chatter of the office staff.

Suddenly, the room's tranquillity was shattered as Nair burst through the grand double doors, clutching the morning's newspapers. His usually composed face was marred with concern. Cyrus looked up, eyebrows raised in silent inquiry.

"You need to see this, Mr. Prime Minister," Nair said urgently, placing the newspaper right in front of Cyrus.

The bold headline screamed back at him: "Karachi's New Era: Hamid Seals Deal with Business Tycoons!" An accompanying photograph depicted a triumphant Hamid, surrounded by influential traders and businessmen, raising a toast.

Cyrus felt a rush of adrenaline. His grip on the newspaper tightened, crumpling the edges. "Why am I learning about this from a newspaper? Why was I not consulted?" he thundered.

Nair hesitated for a split second. "I'm not certain, sir. But it's evident that Hamid acted on his own."

"Get him here. Now!" Cyrus's voice was a low growl, his face a mask of controlled fury.

Cyrus looked up from his desk, where scattered papers told tales of unrest from the presidency towns of Bombay and Calcutta. His piercing eyes met those of Hamid, who had just announced his intention of proclaiming Karachi as the new financial capital.

"Hamid, we can't just declare Karachi as the financial capital without anticipating the ramifications it would have on Bombay and Calcutta," Cyrus stated, his voice deep and measured. The timbre of his voice was such that it could calm a turbulent sea, but not tonight, not with Hamid.

Hamid, a tall figure with a greying beard and sharp features, leaned over the desk, his tone filled with conviction. "Cyrus, the North has always felt sidelined. Karachi has the infrastructure, the passion, and the potential. It's time for a change. It's time we recognize that."

Cyrus, sitting back in his chair, responded, "This is not about North or South, East or West. It's about the entire nation. Proclaiming Karachi without any groundwork or dialogue will create unrest."

Hamid, clearly agitated, retorted, "Bombay and Calcutta have always enjoyed privileges. For once, let the glory be elsewhere. Why can't the North have its due?"

"And it will, Hamid. But not by imposing decisions top-down. We need to engage in discussions, we need consensus. If we force this, the presidency towns will erupt in protest, destabilizing the fragile peace we are trying to establish," Cyrus argued.

The room's temperature seemed to rise. The two stood face to face, their choices poised to sculpt the destiny of a nation.

Hamid's voice was almost a whisper but carried an intensity. "You say you want to unite the country, Cyrus. But sometimes, unity requires making tough choices. Not everyone will be pleased."

Cyrus sighed, rubbing his temples. He could see the sincerity in Hamid's eyes, the genuine desire to see Karachi rise. But the leader in him knew the consequences of a hasty move.

"Hamid, let's commission a study. Let's weigh the pros and cons, and more than that, let's talk to the people of Bombay and Calcutta. Let's not decide their fate without their voice."

Hamid looked into the distance, contemplating. "Fine," he murmured, "but remember, delay doesn't always bring clarity. Sometimes, it just fuels discontent."

As Hamid exited the room, Cyrus sat back, wondering if the unity of this new nation was a dream too ambitious, or perhaps, just a test of their collective resilience.

The news of the heated discussion between Cyrus and Hamid spread like wildfire throughout the corridors of power. The PM's office became a hub of activity, with bureaucrats and politicians trying to gauge the mood and decide where their allegiances should lie.

The next morning, newspapers were filled with headlines discussing the clash of the titans in the capital. Talk of Karachi potentially overshadowing Bombay and Calcutta had stirred a hornet's nest. Street corners, tea stalls, and elite clubs—everywhere one went—the conversation was the same: "Where will India's financial heart lie?"

But while the cities of Bombay and Calcutta bristled with anticipation and protest, Karachi witnessed jubilation. Massive gatherings were organized, where citizens cheered Hamid's proposal, seeing it as a chance for the city, and the North, to finally step out of the shadows.

Panditji called a meeting. Leaders of various factions sat around a long wooden table, the centre of which held a map of India.

Panditji began, "We are at a crossroads. The decision regarding our financial capital isn't merely economic. It's symbolic. It reflects our vision for India."

Ali Bhai, always the voice of reason, added, "We must remember, every decision we make today will set a precedent for the future. We cannot let personal biases cloud our judgment."

Shaukat, supporting his son, argued, "Why is it so hard to see the potential of Karachi? This city has been an epicentre of trade for centuries!"

Patel Sahib, however, was not convinced. "Shaukat, it's not about undermining Karachi's potential. It's about understanding the existing ecosystems of Bombay and Calcutta. Decades, even centuries, of growth can't be shifted overnight."

Gokhale, witnessing the discussion, realized the sensitivity of the issue. As the president of RSD and a staunch Hindu nationalist, his primary focus was India's unity. He interrupted, "Gentlemen, we're missing the point. The question is not which city is better. It's about what's best for India."

All eyes turned to Cyrus, who had remained silent, absorbing everyone's perspectives. With a deep breath, he said, "We need a holistic approach. Let's form a committee representing each city. This committee will engage with economists, urban planners, and most importantly, the citizens. Their insights, combined with data and analysis, should guide our decision."

The room was silent for a moment before erupting in murmurs of agreement.

The political arena might have been cooling, but Cyrus's personal life was reaching boiling point.

January 1948:
The Prime Minister's Residence

Richelle stood by the French window, clutching a telegram in her hand. The telegram had details of her booked passage on a ship to England. Her eyes darted across the sprawling lawns, the nostalgia of a time before the turbulence evident in her gaze.

"Cyrus," she began, her voice trembling but firm, "when we spoke of our dreams, of our life together, it wasn't amidst this political chaos. Every time I hear about a new riot or protest, I fear for your safety. This India... it's not the land I fell in love with."

Cyrus, looking harried and worn from the continuous political meetings, sighed deeply. "Richelle, when I took on this role, I had hopes of a peaceful transition. But the magnitude of the challenges, the hopes and dreams of millions... it's overwhelming."

She turned to face him. "You once spoke of the English countryside, of a quaint home where our future children would play. Now, every day feels like a nightmare, waiting for the next bad news. This isn't the life I envisioned for us."

He stepped closer, reaching out to hold her, but she stepped back. "Richelle, India is in its infancy. She needs guidance, care... and I've been entrusted with that responsibility."

Tears welled up in her eyes. "And what about our responsibility to each other, Cyrus? To the promises we made?"

He tried to find words, the right ones that could bridge the widening gap between them. "Every decision I make, I carry the burden of our dreams and the dreams of this nation. I wish I could give you the peace and life we dreamt of, but right now, India calls."

Richelle's voice broke. "And so, I must answer a call of my own. For peace, for sanity. This telegram," she held it out, "confirms my passage on a ship to England next week."

Cyrus looked at her, disbelief clouding his eyes. "You're leaving?"

She nodded. "I need to find my own path, Cyrus. Maybe, in some other lifetime, our paths would have converged without these divergences."

He reached out, touching her face. "Richelle, please…"

She stepped back, her resolve clear. "Goodbye, Cyrus. I hope you find what you're looking for."

And with that, she walked away, leaving behind an era, a love, and a leader grappling with the trials of his leadership.

Chapter 3

UNYIELDING TIDES

January 5, 1948: New Delhi

The official residence of the home minister, a colonial-era mansion with tall pillars and ornate archways, formed the backdrop of the quiet conversation. The mansion's lush lawns played host to Patel Sahib and Mr. Nair.

Gokhale, looking distinguished in a pristine white kurta, took a deep breath and began, "Patel Sahib, it's been almost six months since independence. Our nation still grapples with its newborn status amidst myriad challenges. And Cyrus, though undeniably gifted, is he ready to face the complexities of this vast nation?"

Patel Sahib responded calmly, "Gokhaleji, your concerns are valid. But let me tell you, in these six months, Cyrus has navigated these treacherous waters with a grace and astuteness that has impressed even his fiercest critics. His understanding of our nation's intricacies has been profound."

Gokhale pondered. "I respect your perspective, but sometimes I feel we are overburdening him. Would it not be an injustice?"

Nair grinned. "Well, Home Minister sahib, every good tea requires the right pressure and time to brew to perfection. Cyrus is no different."

Patel Sahib laughed. "Indeed. And I believe, with our guidance and his own intrinsic capabilities, he will lead us to a future we all envision."

Gokhale nodded. "Very well, we march ahead then, together. For the nation."

The sun began its descent, casting amber hues across the mansion's façade. As the three men walked back into the building, Patel Sahib took out his pocket watch, checking the time. "We shouldn't delay further," he said, adjusting his glasses. "We have that meeting with Cyrus regarding the Constitution Drafting Committee. A foundational moment for our country."

Nair, straightening his tie, chimed in with a wink, "And I've heard that Cyrus's chef has prepared a special dessert for the evening. All the more reason to not be late!"

Gokhale smiled, shaking his head. "Trust you to think of dessert at such a pivotal moment, Nair."

Patel Sahib chuckled. "Let's just say that the promise of a bright future and a delightful dessert await us."

The trio left the mansion, their cars setting off in the direction of the prime minister's residence.

As they approached, the mantle of the upcoming discussions was on their minds, but the camaraderie between them offered a comforting reassurance.

Upon arriving at the stately residence, they were greeted by Cyrus, Shaukat, Hamid, Ali Bhai and Panditji, who ushered them into a meeting room, its walls adorned with paintings. The atmosphere was one of serious anticipation, as they all knew the importance of the discussions that lay ahead.

Gokhale, taking a moment to scan the room, addressed Cyrus with a tone of respectful urgency. "Before we delve into the intricacies of the Constitution Drafting Committee, we must address the immediate need for cabinet expansion," he said. "It's been six months, Cyrus, and the burden of governance cannot rest on your shoulders alone. You need a robust team."

Patel Sahib, nodding in agreement, leaned forward, his experienced eyes meeting Cyrus's. "Gokhale is right," he said. "A strong cabinet is essential for effective governance. I suggest we consider the following names:"

Vikram Joshi – Defence Minister: Recommended by Panditji, Vikram was a tall, broad-shouldered man, with sharp eyes that always seemed to be assessing and evaluating situations. A decorated army officer, Joshi had an air of authority, yet his voice was always calm and measured. Having served in the army during the turbulent times of World War II, he had an acute understanding of war strategies and the importance of a fortified defence for the nation.

Dr. Rao – National Security Advisor: Patel Sahib's choice, Dr. Rao was a stark contrast to Vikram Joshi. Of average height and build, with salt-and-pepper hair, he wore thick glasses that gave him a scholarly appearance. And rightfully so, for he was a leading academic before being brought into the fold of governance. Known for his analytical mind, he had written several papers on global geopolitics and security threats. He had an uncanny ability to look at security issues with a 360-degree perspective.

Nalini Sen – External Affairs Minister: The surprise pick recommended by Panditji was Nalini Sen. Nalini, with her sharp features and commanding presence, had been British India's ambassador to various nations before independence. Fluent in six languages and with a PhD in international relations, she was known to mesmerize her audience with her eloquence. More than that, she had a natural flair for diplomacy, often able to defuse tense situations with her tact and grace.

Vishwanathan Pradhan – Special Advisor to the PM on Foreign Affairs: Mr. Pradhan was a graduate of the London School of Economics and brought with him a wealth of experience, having served as an ambassador to multiple countries. His insights into global economic trends and foreign policy were recognized internationally. His distinguished career and academic credentials spoke volumes of his capability to advise on matters that would shape the nation's foreign policy.

As the names were proposed, Cyrus listened intently, weighing each suggestion. He knew that each individual would bring unique strengths to the cabinet, forming a collective that would guide the nation through its formative years.

Cyrus, leaning against the mahogany desk, looked pensively at Ali Bhai, Panditji, and Patel Sahib. "With new names being added to the cabinet, I wonder why none of you have shown interest in being part of it," he inquired, his voice tinged with curiosity and a hint of concern.

Ali Bhai, his expression solemn, responded in a measured tone, "Cyrus, our absence from the cabinet was a foundational condition for avoiding the partition of our nation. We couldn't risk any perception of power being centralized in the hands of a few, especially not among us. It's a matter of maintaining the people's trust."

Cyrus listened intently as Ali Bhai continued, "The Muslim community was apprehensive about Panditji and Patel Sahib holding positions of power, just as the Hindu community was wary of me.

We have to respect these sentiments to maintain the delicate balance we've achieved."

There was a silence in the room, the complexity of communal harmony hanging in the air. Cyrus broke the silence, a note of realization in his voice. "You three are like the Trimurti of our government," he said, a respectful acknowledgement of their roles.

Panditji, with a light smile, replied, "Perhaps in a way we are, Cyrus. But our roles are now more about guiding from the shadows than leading from the front. The nation needs fresh faces in the cabinet, unburdened by the past and looking towards the future."

After listening attentively to the proposed names for cabinet expansion, Cyrus nodded in agreement, a sense of trust and respect evident in his demeanour. "I trust your judgment and the choices you have made for the cabinet expansion," he affirmed, his voice carrying a tone of decisiveness. "I will personally meet each of the three candidates you've suggested. Let's ensure we bring in individuals who are not only capable but also dedicated to the vision of a progressive and united India."

Turning to Nair, Cyrus instructed, "Please begin the necessary procedures to induct them into the cabinet. We need to move swiftly and efficiently on this."

With the matter of cabinet expansion settled, Cyrus redirected the focus of the meeting. "Now, let us proceed to the next critical agenda – the drafting of our Constitution," he announced, shifting gears to address the monumental task at hand.

The drafting of the Constitution was not just a legal formality; it was the creation of the very soul of the nation, a document that would define the identity, values, and aspirations of the newly independent India.

Cyrus continued, "The Constitution will be the foundation upon which our democratic ideals are built. It needs to reflect our diversity, protect the rights of every citizen, and guide us towards a future of equality and justice."

Panditji, leaning forward with an assertive energy, added, "Gentlemen, we need to recognize that India is not England. We're a tapestry of languages, cultures, and religions. We've been under the yoke of the British for too long. We can't use their lack of a written constitution as an excuse for not having our own."

Shaukat countered, "But England's system has evolved over centuries. They have precedents, common law, and statutes that guide them. Why do we need a static document that might chain us down?"

Cyrus interjected, "It's precisely because we are diverse that we need a constitution. It will be the beacon that will guide our ship through the tumultuous seas of democracy. This document will be our moral compass, ensuring that each citizen is treated with dignity and respect."

Patel Sahib, intervened, "While I respect England's legacy, we must carve our own path. But we must also be cautious. A constitution, if not crafted with precision, can become a double-edged sword."

Ali Bhai leaned back in his chair, stroking his beard. "The Quran is our guiding light. Why do we need another document? Won't that dilute our principles?"

Cyrus, realizing the seriousness of the situation, took a deep breath. "Our constitution will not be a replacement for our religious or moral teachings. Instead, it will be a reflection of our collective spirit, an affirmation of our unity in diversity. Our diverse backgrounds should be our strength, not our weakness."

It was then that Cyrus made his boldest move. "I propose we form a committee to draft this constitution. And I believe Dr. Dharmadhikari, with his unique background and legal prowess, should head it. I have already requested him to do the needful. Have set up a meeting tomorrow with him. Request everyone's presence."

Murmurs filled the room. Dharmadhikari, despite his brilliance, was from a lower caste—an unpalatable choice for many in the room. Gokhale, ever the diplomat, chimed in, "It is not one's birth but one's abilities that should determine their place in society. Dharmadhikari has shown time and again his acumen and dedication."

Cyrus added, "It's symbolic. Having someone like Dharmadhikari at the helm will send a message that in our new India, everyone, irrespective of their birth, has an equal stake."

Ali Bhai sighed. "If this constitution binds us together, rather than tears us apart, then I will support it. But remember, it's a gamble."

Panditji nodded. "Indeed, a gamble. But one worth taking for the future of India."

The next morning, the double doors to the PM's office creaked open. A junior aide walked in, announcing, "Dr. Dharmadhikari has arrived, sir."

A tall, slender figure, Dharmadhikari carried himself with an air of quiet authority. His skin bore the sun-kissed hue of someone who had spent years toiling in the fields of Maharashtra before rising through the ranks of academia and law. His eyes, sharp and observant, had a deep-set, thoughtful look—always scrutinizing, always assessing. A neatly trimmed moustache sat above a determined mouth, often breaking into a smile that radiated warmth and understanding.

His attire was a blend of traditional and modern; he usually wore crisply starched white kurta-pyjamas paired with a handwoven Nehru jacket. A pair of spectacles with rounded frames rested on his prominent nose, which he often removed to polish when in deep thought. His hands were a testament to his journey, slightly rough from the years of manual labour yet refined from years of wielding a pen and pouring over legal manuscripts. A hush settled over the room as Dharmadhikari made his entrance.

Cyrus rose from his seat, extending a hand. "Ah, Dharmadhikari, just the man we've been waiting for. Come, take a seat."

As Dharmadhikari settled in, the room seemed to adjust to his calm yet assertive presence. The meeting had officially begun, and the fate of a nation lay, in part, in the hands of this self-made man.

Dr. Dharmadhikari sat across Cyrus. There was humility in his posture. Being appointed as the chairman of the Constitution Drafting Committee was not just an honour, but it was also a monumental responsibility.

"Prime Minister, I am deeply honoured by your trust in appointing me for this task," Dr. Dharmadhikari began, his voice steady yet tinged with the enormity of the challenge ahead.

"However, I must request more time for this endeavour. India's vast expanse, encompassing myriad regions, customs, traditions, and a history spanning over a thousand years, cannot be hastily encapsulated in a single document. To draft a constitution that truly reflects the soul of our nation will require careful consideration and time."

Cyrus, who had been listening intently, nodded in understanding. "Dr. Dharmadhikari, your request for time is well-founded. This process is indeed crucial and demands perfection. The constitution we draft will not just be a document; it will be the guiding light for our nation's future generations. Take the time you need to ensure it embodies the principles of justice, equality, and unity that we stand for."

Dharmadhikari, having just taken a sip of his tea, locked eyes with Ali Bhai. The room fell silent, waiting for the impending debate that was about to unfold.

"Why do we need such a document, Dharmadhikari?" Ali Bhai began, his voice laced with scepticism. "The British ruled us for centuries without a written constitution. Why should we tie ourselves down with written words and lose the fluidity and adaptability we've always possessed?"

Dharmadhikari, setting down his cup with precision, replied, "Ali Bhai, the British had an empire, and they managed it the way they saw fit. We are building a nation. A diverse, vast, and intricate nation, filled with myriad beliefs, customs, and languages. We need a framework to ensure that every citizen, regardless of their background, has equal rights and is protected from any possible tyranny."

Ali Bhai leaned forward. "But wouldn't such a document become a tool in the hands of those who might want to wield power unfairly?"

Smiling, Dharmadhikari responded, "That's precisely why we need it. A well-drafted constitution will safeguard against that very misuse. It will set boundaries, ensuring no one, no matter how powerful, can overstep."

Ali Bhai looked contemplative, nodding slowly. "I see your point. But remember, it must reflect every voice, every heart in this land, not just those who shout the loudest."

Dharmadhikari, his eyes earnest, assured, "That, Ali Bhai, is precisely the mission."

As the intense debate over the constitution raged on, Mr. Nair walked in with a cup of chai. "You know, in my village, when two people can't agree, they sit down with a cup of chai. By the time they finish, they always have an answer." He winked. "Maybe we need bigger cups."

In the coming days, Dharmadhikari set up his team, pulling in legal minds from across the country, representing various regions, religions, and backgrounds. The aim was clear—the Constitution had to be a mirror reflecting the true face of India in all its diverse glory.

As weeks turned into months, the committee members huddled together in numerous sessions, sometimes stretching deep into the night. The nation watched with bated breath, hopeful yet anxious. There were issues of representation, the rights of states, the place of religion, and most critically, the rights and duties of citizens.

However, the challenges weren't just confined within those four walls. Outside, the RSD voiced concerns about ensuring that the Hindu ethos wasn't drowned out. Meanwhile, the Muslim Quam was keen to ensure that their rights weren't trampled upon in a country where they were a minority.

Cyrus, in a meeting with Gokhale, expressed his concerns. "The Constitution needs to stand the test of time. It has to be a living document, evolving with our nation."

Gokhale nodded. "You're right. But it's also crucial to ensure that while it stands firm on principles, it provides room for flexibility. A too rigid system will crack under pressure."

As his team embarked on the journey of drafting the Constitution, questions lingered in the air.

Could a single document withstand the pressures of diverse religions, castes, and regions? Would it be able to unite a nation with such varied histories and identities under one flag? These were not just theoretical queries but real challenges that would test the resilience and inclusivity of the Constitution. Only time would reveal if this cornerstone of Indian democracy could hold up to the aspirations of its people and the complexities of its societal fabric. The task was herculean, but the hope was that this Constitution would not only survive the test of time but also emerge as a beacon of India's unity in diversity.

November 1948: Bombay

A city was on the rise from the ashes of a devastating earthquake. The air smelled of sea salt and ambition. The chug of boats, the clamour of construction, and the distant hum of tramcars formed a rhythmic symphony. It was a city that had learned to build over its tragedies.

Cyrus stepped into the grand hall of the University of Bombay, his steps echoing in the vast space, magnifying the charge of administration he felt. A massive wooden table gleamed under the chandeliers, surrounded by eminent academicians, all awaiting the prime minister.

The University of Bombay, rebuilt in the aftermath of the devastating earthquake, stood tall and resplendent against the backdrop of the Arabian Sea. Its Gothic-style architecture, combined with elements of Indian aesthetics, symbolized a nation rising from the ashes, eager to meld its rich history with modern aspirations.

Inside a grand, wood-panelled conference room, an air of anticipation hung heavy. Cyrus, the young prime minister, was about to convene a meeting with the nation's top scientific and academic minds. The vast oval table, polished to a mirror sheen, reflected the faces of those who were shaping India's intellectual renaissance.

Seated there were Dr. Varma, the renowned physicist; Prof. Mehta, the historian whose work on ancient Indian sciences was celebrated worldwide; Dr. Joshi, a nuclear scientist recently returned from Europe; and Prof. Krishnan, an educator with revolutionary ideas about pedagogy.

"We are at a juncture," began Cyrus, scanning the faces around him, "where our past can illuminate our path forward. Our ancestors were pioneers in various fields. Now, in 1948, post-independence, post-earthquake, it's our turn to etch our mark."

Prof. Mehta nodded. "Indeed, Mr. Prime Minister. We must look back to move forward.

Nalanda was the pinnacle of academic excellence in its time. How do we translate that spirit, that quest for knowledge, into our current scenario?"

Dr. Joshi, ever the pragmatist, interjected, "While history serves as a guide, the world today is looking at the atom and the stars. We must invest in nuclear research and space technology."

"Exactly," chimed in Dr. Varma. "I envision an Indian Space Organization, one that doesn't just emulate others but pioneers its own path."

Cyrus, listening intently, said, "And that's why we're here, at the University of Bombay, the emblem of our resurgence."

Prof. Krishnan, adjusting his spectacles, added, "Our curriculum must reflect not just the sciences but also the humanities. A holistic education, steeped in ethics, will shape the citizens of tomorrow."

As discussions about space research and nuclear energy slowly concluded, Cyrus unveiled a blueprint. It wasn't just any blueprint but the one representing a vision for India's future in education.

With a sense of reverence, he spread it across the table. It showed a sprawling campus, state-of-the-art labs, vast libraries, and spacious lecture halls. The name at the top read: *Indian Institute of Engineering, Medical and Science, Nalanda.*

"Nalanda," Cyrus began, his voice filled with emotion, "once stood as the beacon of knowledge, attracting scholars from all corners of the world. It's only fitting that our first endeavour in shaping the future of engineering education be rooted there."

Dr. Joshi's eyes sparkled with excitement. "Rekindling Nalanda's glory with modern engineering prowess is a masterstroke, Mr. Prime Minister! We would not just be building an institution but reviving a legacy."

Prof. Mehta, always the historian, leaned forward. "The world knew Nalanda as the bedrock of education, where thousands came to quench their thirst for knowledge. Reviving it in this form is a symbolic gesture that India is reclaiming its place on the global academic stage."

Prof. Krishnan added thoughtfully, "Imagine the symbolism! Students from all over the world arriving in Nalanda once again, not for religious or philosophical studies of ancient times but for the cutting-edge engineering courses of the modern world."

Dr. Varma smiled. "And amidst those ancient ruins, we'll have futuristic classrooms The juxtaposition of the old and the new!"

Cyrus nodded. "We'll ensure the institute blends seamlessly with Nalanda's ethos. Our architecture will pay homage to its history while representing India's forward march."

The ambience of the hall was formal yet lively. There was an air of expectancy. People knew that the decisions made today would shape the course of their nation's intellectual future.

Suddenly, the doors to the hall swung open, causing heads to turn in their direction. A sea of students, professors, and administrators made way for Mrs. Chatterjee, the media advisor to the prime minister. The look on her face suggested urgency.

She approached the table, handing Cyrus a sealed envelope. "Sir, my apologies for interrupting, but this couldn't wait."

The room was thick with anticipation. Cyrus, looking slightly taken aback by the interruption, carefully opened the envelope and quickly scanned its contents. The colour drained slightly from his face as he comprehended the gravity of the message.

"Is everything all right, sir?" asked Prof. Mehta, the dean of the university, standing beside him.

Cyrus took a deep breath, his demeanour transitioning from the calm, collected statesman to that of a leader faced with a crisis.

"It appears," he began slowly, "that we have a situation brewing in Mewad. The maharani is attempting a secession. She wants her son, Maharaja Rajyavardhan, to be proclaimed prince of the princely state and doesn't wish to integrate with the Indian Union."

Whispers spread through the hall. Mewad was one of the wealthiest princely states, and its integration was crucial to the nation's unification and stability.

Mrs. Chatterjee added, her voice carrying an unmistakable note of concern, "Early reports suggest that the maharani has garnered significant local support. She has also supposedly hired foreign mercenaries to train her private guards."

The room was charged with tension. The idea of fragmented nation-states within the Union could prove disastrous. Cyrus, processing the information, spoke in a resolute tone, "We must address this with tact and diplomacy. But we should also be prepared to stand firm on our principles."

Mrs. Chatterjee nodded. "The Prime Minister's Office is setting up a task force. Your guidance will be crucial."

Cyrus, acknowledging the intensity of the situation, stated, "Then let's convene immediately. This nation was born out of unity and sacrifice;

we cannot let individual aspirations undermine our collective dream."

Ending the meeting abruptly, Cyrus, Mrs. Chatterjee, and a few key advisors quickly exited the hall, determined to confront this new challenge head-on.

Chapter 4

ECHOES OF MEWAD

November 1, 1948: Mewad Palace

Mewad, once the seat of a formidable dynasty, now found itself at a crossroads. Situated in the northern reaches of the country, the city was a blend of antiquity and modernity. While ancient palaces and temples painted a picture of a bygone era, the markets buzzed with the latest goods and the promise of a thriving future. Emerald lakes dotted its geography, and the distant mountains loomed, watching over this prized city like silent guardians.

The city had always been insulated from the political upheavals of the mainland thanks to its natural fortifications and the shrewd diplomacy of its rulers. This was until the winds of change blowing through the Indian subcontinent in 1947 reached its gates.

At the heart of the city's main market, a massive stage had been set up. Overlooking the gathering was the grand statue of the city's founder, Maharaja Pratapvardhan. Thousands had congregated, the air palpable with a mix of excitement, curiosity, and uncertainty.

Maharani Udayamati, the widow of the late maharaja and the mother of young Maharaja Rajyavardhan, stepped onto the stage. Draped in a regal saree of deep blue with intricate gold embroidery, she epitomized grace and authority. Her eyes, sharp and discerning, surveyed the crowd. She was known for her keen intellect, having played a crucial role in the court's politics even when her husband was alive. The large diamond tiara on her head symbolized the opulence of Mewad, but it was her aura that commanded unwavering respect.

She began, her voice clear and strong, echoing across the market square, "People of Mewad! For generations, our ancestors have built this great city, nurturing it with their blood, sweat, and tears. Today, we stand at a precipice. The winds from Delhi speak of unification, of a singular identity. But we must ask—at what cost?"

The crowd listened intently, hanging on to every word. She continued, "Mewad has thrived because we've always been masters of our destiny. Now, they ask us to be a mere page in a vast book. But aren't we a tale grand enough to have our own tome?"

The crowd murmured in agreement.

The maharani, a vision of elegance, resumed. "This land, its stories, its heritage… it belongs to us. Our son will lead us, as his ancestors did."

The maharaja, bolstered by the support of seventeen other princely states, declared defiantly, "We stand united. Our legacy is not up for negotiation."

"Maharaja Rajyavardhan, our future and hope, will ensure that Mewad remains the shimmering jewel of this land, independent and proud. We owe this to our forefathers and to our future generations." The maharani's voice, amplified by a rudimentary loudspeaker system, carried across the square, filled with passionate fervour. "Mewad has always been a land of pride! We have our history, our traditions, and our pride. Why should we let outsiders decide our fate?"

Cheers erupted from the crowd, echoing her sentiment.

"We have seen our brothers and sisters in other princely states being stripped of their identity, their traditions trampled underfoot in the name of a united India," she continued, her voice dripping with contempt. "But not us! We will resist! We will fight!" She pointed dramatically at a shop flying the Indian flag. "Boycott them! Those who align with this so-called united India are traitors to Mewad!"

With those words, chaos ensued. Groups of agitated supporters stormed shops and restaurants showing any allegiance to India. Windows were shattered, goods were thrown onto the streets, and fires began to break out. The city's few government buildings were besieged, their façades defaced and their interiors ransacked.

Through it all, the maharani stood on the dais, her expression one of cold satisfaction. The seed of rebellion had been sown, and Mewad was in the throes of dissent.

As she concluded, the market erupted in applause, punctuated by chants supporting her stance. Maharani Udayamati, with a nod of acknowledgement, made her exit, leaving behind a city united in its aspiration but standing on the brink of a defining confrontation.

In a lavish chamber illuminated by chandeliers, Maharaja Rajyavardhan convened a meeting with leaders of the other defiant princely states. The air was thick with tension and uncertainty.

The maharaja's aide, his voice laced with worry, whispered to him, "Sahib, can we stand against Delhi?"

He responded, his voice unwavering, "Our ancestors built these lands. I cannot let their legacy be overshadowed. We will remain united."

A prince from a neighbouring state, Ranveer of Purnagiri, voiced his concerns. "We must also think of our people. If a conflict erupts, they will suffer."

The maharaja's best friend, Prince Akhtar of Nadirpur, interjected, "Then let's present a united front. Let the central government know we stand together."

As the night wore on, the eighteen princely states formed an alliance: The United Sovereigns of India.

As evening approached, and the fires in the market began to wane, the news of the day's events rapidly reached the central government, setting the stage for a tense meeting at the prime minister's residence.

In Delhi, the stress was palpable. The grandeur of the prime minister's residence was in stark contrast to the tension that filled the room.

Panditji's fingers drummed nervously on the mahogany table. Gokhale had worry lines creasing his forehead. Ali Bhai was the first to break the silence. "Perhaps a middle ground can be found. Limited autonomy for Mewad might appease them."

Gokhale shot up, his voice rising. "Ali Bhai, you know as well as I do that it's a slippery slope. If we give Mewad autonomy, every princely state will want the same. It's a recipe for anarchy."

Nair, adjusting his glasses, added, "Gokhaleji is right. It's not just about Mewad. We're crafting the very soul of our nation here."

Mrs. Chatterjee interjected, "But we cannot ignore the sentiments of the people there. The maharani has considerable influence. We need a solution that doesn't tear the fabric of our fledgling democracy."

Shortly thereafter, Mrs. Chatterjee's secretary entered the room, a file clutched tightly in her hand. "Sir, our intelligence has just informed us about the maharani's next move," she said, addressing Cyrus. "She is convening a secret meeting with seventeen other princes. They are planning to make a united declaration of independence."

Panditji sighed, running a hand through his hair. "Perhaps a dialogue is in order. Maybe if we sit with the maharani, we can find common ground. Cyrus, what are your thoughts?"

Cyrus, trying to mediate, sought to bring calm. "Gentlemen, we need unity at this time, not disagreements." His eyes darted to Patel Sahib, who had been uncharacteristically silent throughout the discussion. The old statesman was deep in thought, his eyes focused on some distant point.

Cyrus gently probed. "Patel Sahib, your counsel has always been our guiding light. We need your wisdom."

Patel Sahib took a deep breath. "Mewad is not just another princely state. It's symbolic. If Mewad falls, it sends a message that our vision of a unified India is negotiable." He paused, letting his words sink in, before dropping the bombshell. "We need a surgical strike. We nip this in the bud."

A stunned silence enveloped the room. The term 'surgical strike', aggressive and final, was not one often used in the corridors of the prime minister's residence. Panditji's eyes widened in disbelief, Gokhale looked as if he had been slapped, and Ali Bhai sat back, shocked.

Cyrus took a deep breath. "While I respect your perspective, Patel Sahib, we must weigh all our options carefully. This is a decision that will echo through the annals of history."

Patel Sahib, stern-faced, responded, "Sometimes, to build a nation, tough decisions have to be made. History will judge us not by our intentions but by our actions." The echo of his words hung heavily in the room as the leaders grappled with the monumental decision before them.

Patel Sahib said firmly, "There's only one man who can handle this situation and ensure Mewad stays with India. General Singh."

The name commanded immediate respect. General Harjinder Singh was a towering figure, both literally and figuratively. Standing at over six feet tall, this firm Sikh, with his dense beard and piercing eyes, had an aura of command that few could match. His reputation wasn't just limited to India; even the British, during their rule, had often sung praises of his strategic acumen and courage. Decorated with numerous awards for his bravery in World War II, Singh was a soldier's soldier—a man who would lay down his life for his country without a second thought.

As the tension in the room grew palpable, Cyrus's voice cut through, unwavering and determined. "Arrange a meeting with General Singh. I need to see him immediately," he directed his secretary.

The scene transitioned subtly, as though the problems of one evening had melted into the fresh hope of the next morning. Birds chirped their morning tunes, and the sun rose slowly over the PM's residence, casting a golden glow.

The rhythmic thud of boots on the gravel announced the arrival of the much-awaited guest. The doors swung open to reveal General Singh in his pristine army uniform adorned with various medals that glistened in the morning light. With a brisk pace, he approached the prime minister, his sharp eyes never wavering. Stopping a few feet away, he saluted crisply. "Jai Hind, Mr. Prime Minister," his voice boomed. "You've summoned me. How can I serve the nation?"

Cyrus, acknowledging the salute with a nod, gestured for the general to sit. The room was filled with some of the nation's most influential figures, but with General Singh's entry, a new sense of direction and purpose felt imminent.

Before the discussion commenced, the general's voice was firm, "Mr. Prime Minister, if we are to discuss strategies on Mewad, I request a private conversation."

Cyrus glanced around the room. Ali Bhai's face showed evident concern, Panditji was as calm as ever, but the undercurrent of worry was unmistakable. Patel Sahib, usually the pillar of decisiveness, now appeared contemplative.

"I understand the sensitivity of the situation, General," Cyrus began, "but you can trust the people in this room."

The general shook his head. "It's not a matter of trust, Mr. Prime Minister. It's a matter of confidentiality. Even walls have ears."

Ali Bhai stood up gracefully. "I respect your wishes, General. I'll wait outside." Panditji, though hesitant, followed suit. Patel Sahib took a moment longer, his eyes locking with Cyrus's, communicating a silent promise to support any decision that was made.

Cyrus then turned to Gokhale and Nair. Nair was shifting his weight from one foot to another, looking slightly uncomfortable, but Gokhale stood firm, awaiting instructions.

"Gokhale, Nair, I want both of you here," Cyrus asserted.

The room was thick with anticipation. General Singh waited until the door clicked shut behind Patel Sahib before he spoke. "Mewad is a tinderbox, Mr. Prime Minister. One wrong move and it could ignite a fire that engulfs the nation. But we also cannot let it become a blueprint for other princely states."

Nair chimed in, "I've been hearing whispers, General. Whispers that suggest there's more at play than just the pride of the maharani. Foreign interests, perhaps?"

General Singh nodded. "Exactly. The British may have left, but their interests haven't. We must tread carefully. A show of force may be necessary, but it should be our last resort."

Gokhale suggested, "We need a multi-pronged approach. Diplomacy, intelligence, and force, in that order."

Cyrus, taking in the perspectives of these trusted advisors, felt the onus of authority heavily. "All right," he declared, "we'll start with diplomacy. We send an envoy to Mewad. If that doesn't work, we gather intel. And if everything fails, then General Singh, I trust you and your men to do what is necessary to protect the integrity of our nation."

General Singh saluted. "We stand ready, Mr. Prime Minister."

November 3, 1948: Mewad City

The Mewad market, once a bustling hub of commerce and camaraderie, now stood divided. The once-unified hum of haggling and bartering now sounded more like disjointed notes of discord. Flags bearing the insignia of the maharani's envisioned independent state fluttered from some shops while others displayed the tricolour, symbolizing their desire to be a part of a newly independent India. Directly across from each other, Rajiv's tea stall bore the tricolour while Ahmed's textile store was adorned with the maharani's flags. Every morning, Rajiv would serve tea, commenting loudly about the benefits of a united India while Ahmed would retaliate by showcasing fabrics that bore patterns of the maharani's insignia. Their once-friendly banter had now taken on a more acrimonious tone.

In the middle of this divide was Iqbal's grocery store, which refrained from displaying any flags. Iqbal believed in harmony and wished for the town to remain united. He became the unofficial mediator, often trying to calm heated discussions and reminding everyone of the times when the town had stood together in solidarity.

Amidst this tumult, young love blossomed. Anika, a staunch supporter of the maharani, found herself drawn to Sameer, who dreamt of a united India. Their secret meetings, away from the prying eyes of the market, became the stuff of local legends. Their love story was a beacon of hope for many, symbolizing that unity and love could overcome even the most profound differences.

The atmosphere in Mewad's market was a microcosm of the larger ideological war brewing in the princely state.

It was a city on the edge, every corner telling a story of division, hope, resilience, and anticipation.

November 4, 1948:
The Prime Minister's Residence

The atmosphere was starkly different. The room was cloaked in heavy tension when Mrs. Chatterjee entered. Her face, usually composed and unreadable, betrayed a hint of nervousness…

"Sir, the maharani has not only refused to meet our envoy, but she's also given a rather audacious proposition," she informed crisply, her eyes darting between the prime minister and the general.

Cyrus leaned forward in his chair, his fingers interlocked, his brow furrowed. "What is it?" he demanded.

"She suggests that we can open a diplomatic embassy in Mewad. Even offered a property at a reduced rent." Mrs. Chatterjee's voice quivered slightly as she anticipated the reaction.

For a brief moment, there was complete silence, as if the room itself had inhaled sharply. Then, the storm broke.

"This audacity!" thundered Cyrus, his usually calm demeanour displaced by a rare show of fury. "She sees us as a foreign nation in our own land?!"

General Singh stood ramrod straight, waiting for orders, his military discipline evident in his stillness. He looked directly at Cyrus, his eyes sharp and resolute.

Cyrus met General Singh's gaze. "General, I think it's time."

General Singh nodded, understanding the seriousness of the situation. "Sir, are we initiating 'Operation Golden Sparrow'?"

"We are," Cyrus affirmed, his anger now channelled into a determined resolve. "We cannot let the dreams of a united India be compromised by a few rogue elements."

Mrs. Chatterjee and Nair exchanged glances. This operation was known to few within the highest echelons of government. It was a carefully crafted strategy to deal with secessionist movements swiftly and decisively, ensuring minimal civilian casualties.

Nair adjusted his glasses and chimed in, "We need to handle this carefully. The international community will be watching."

Cyrus leaned back, the onus of leadership evident in his posture. "General, ensure the operation is swift and clean. We cannot afford a prolonged conflict."

General Singh saluted. "You have my word, sir. India will remain united."

As he turned to leave, Mrs. Chatterjee added, "May the winds be in our favour." A silent prayer, a hope that this operation would steer the nation towards unity and away from impending chaos.

As the last words were uttered in the prime minister's residence, a profound sense of resolution settled in the room.

November 10, 1948:
Undisclosed Location, Mewad

The room was dimly lit. There was an old wooden table in the centre, overburdened with maps, charts, and documents. Several cups of chai sit alongside them.

General Singh stood at the head of the table. Surrounding the table were his top commanders, men and women who'd been through the grit of war, their faces carved with experiences and responsibilities.

General Singh broke the silence. "We have been entrusted with a mission of national importance. The fate of Mewad and the stability of our young nation rest on our shoulders."

Commander Rajan, a stocky man with a scar running down his left cheek, spoke up. "Sir, we've been surveying Mewad for days. The fort is impenetrable from the front. The maharani knows she has the upper hand."

Lieutenant Thappa, the youngest amongst them but a tactical genius, slid a blueprint forward. "There's an old aqueduct that runs underneath the fort, dating back to the Mughal era. We've confirmed it's largely unguarded."

General Singh nodded, appreciating the intel. "This will be the entry for the Night Sparrows. But we need distractions, diversions to keep their main forces occupied."

Another commander, Captain Rana, chimed in, "Our intelligence suggests the fort has recently fortified its armoury. If we can sabotage it, it would cripple their defences."

The discussion grew intense as strategies were formed, risks assessed, and roles assigned. Every minor detail was considered, from the wind direction on the night of the operation to the psyche of the maharani's guards.

As the hours rolled by, the room became a hub of synchronized planning. General Singh concluded, "We will give Mewad its dawn. Operation Golden Sparrow is a go!"

A young lieutenant asked, "Sir, why this name for the operation?"

Captain Singh smiled. "Mewad is known as the City of Gold. Its golden spires and rich history make it invaluable. We're not just capturing a palace, we're reclaiming a legacy."

Under the supervision of General Singh, a specialized team was formed, handpicked for their expertise in guerrilla warfare, stealth operations, and diplomacy. Two units were at play: the 'Night Sparrows'—a covert ops team, and 'Dawn Guardians'—a larger infantry group for backup.

November 11, 1948: Mewad

As dawn broke, the majestic Mewad Palace was surrounded.

On a moonless night, the Night Sparrows, dressed in all black, commenced the operation.

Their first task was to neutralize the guards silently without raising any alarms. Each member was armed with silenced weapons and a traditional dagger. They spread out, taking cover behind the fort's high walls and strategically placed statues.

While two members of the team disabled the communication lines, ensuring that no external help could be summoned, others planted explosives at key infrastructure points as a contingency.

The next step was to enter the fort's main hall. Using grappling hooks, two members ascended the walls, taking out the sentries on the watchtowers. Once the outer perimeter was secure, the rest of the team entered through the underground tunnel.

Inside, they encountered minimal resistance, thanks to the element of surprise. The few guards present were quickly subdued.

The Dawn Guardians, after receiving a signal, started their march towards the fort, ensuring that no reinforcements from the town reached the fort.

The maharaja, awakened by the rhythmic thumping of marching boots, realized that something was not right.

The showdown was intense.

Upon reaching the inner sanctum, the Night Sparrows found themselves face to face with the maharani and her closest aides. But instead of a confrontation, General Singh, who had joined the covert team for this crucial moment, stepped forward. He made a passionate plea for unity and the vision of a collective future.

The grand hall of the palace saw Captain Singh confront the maharani. "Your Highness, I urge you, think of your people. Integrate with India and preserve the peace."

The tension in the room was palpable. Swords drawn, guards on edge, every second felt like an eternity. Then, much to everyone's surprise, the maharani signalled her men to lower their weapons.

As the sun began to dip, casting a golden hue upon the horizon, the fort's flag was lowered, replaced by the tricolour of India. The mission was accomplished.

Exhausted, battle-scarred but undefeated, the soldiers gathered in the central courtyard. The fort might have been a maze, the mission might have felt like penetrating another country, but in those gruelling twelve hours, they had reclaimed a part of their homeland.

The general looked up at the fluttering flag, his face illuminated by the setting sun. "For the nation," he whispered, his voice hoarse but filled with pride.

The majestic palace of Mewad stood tall amidst the vast landscapes of the princely state, its spires touching the cerulean sky. But today, its grandeur was overshadowed by a sombre atmosphere. The central courtyard, usually bustling with activities and laughter, was filled with soldiers, their uniforms crisp and their demeanour unyielding.

Inside the opulent throne room, Maharaja Rajyavardhan stood, his usually resplendent robes now slightly dishevelled. Around him, his loyalists and ministers whispered urgently, their faces etched with worry.

The massive wooden doors of the throne room were thrown open, and in marched General Singh, flanked by his top commanders. The clinking of their boots against the marble floor echoed ominously in the vast chamber.

The maharaja's eyes locked onto General Singh's. There was a challenge in the former's gaze but also an unmistakable hint of defeat.

"Maharaja Rajyavardhan," General Singh's voice boomed, "you are under arrest for treason against the state of India. I have orders from the prime minister to send you and your family to Burma, where you will be living in exile."

As the maharaja was handcuffed, his mother, the defiant maharani, watched from the balcony above, her eyes burning with tears of rage and sorrow.

The word spread like wildfire among the princely states about the fall of Mewad's monarch. There was a scramble, a hurried rush of messengers on horses, and soon, an assembly of seventeen anxious princes was called in the heart of Delhi.

December 15, 1948:
The Prime Minister's Office, New Delhi

The vast assembly hall, adorned with ornate chandeliers and plush carpets, was filled with a nervous energy. The princes, in their regal attires, whispered among themselves, their eyes darting to the entrance every so often.

The door finally opened, and in walked Prime Minister Cyrus Engineer, his stature commanding respect.

Cyrus began, "Esteemed leaders, our actions in Mewad were not against its people but against the act of defiance that could tear our young nation apart. However, I recognize the value each of your states brings to this union."

A prince from the East, dressed in rich silks, voiced the collective concern. "Prime Minister, our traditions, our legacies—will they be overshadowed by this new India?"

Cyrus reassured, "Our aim is not dominance but unity. While we progress as one nation, we will ensure your unique histories and cultures remain celebrated."

As Prime Minister Engineer made his reassuring address, other leaders present in the room also felt compelled to provide their perspectives to the nervous assembly of princes.

Panditji stood up and cleared his throat. "Esteemed leaders, India's freedom came with countless sacrifices, and now, as a nascent nation, we must move forward hand in hand. Your rich histories and legacies are what make India—the India we so deeply love and cherish. We are not here to rob you of your traditions but to integrate them into our shared dream."

Gokhale added, "Maharaja Rajyavardhan's defiance was a challenge to our sovereignty, not to the cultural essence of Mewad or any other princely state. Had he chosen dialogue over dissent, the outcome might have been different. I urge you all to consider this and understand that our actions were born out of necessity, not malice."

Patel Sahib emphasized the importance of unity. "In this room, I see India. Each of you represents a part of our great nation. But remember, while a finger alone can be easily broken, a fist is unyielding. Let's come together, not as separate entities but as one united force for the betterment of our people."

Mr. Nair, trying to lighten the atmosphere a bit, joked, "With so many royals in one room, this could easily be the most lavish wedding of the century."

The comment earned a few chuckles from the princes, helping to diffuse some of the tension.

The room had witnessed moments of stress and passion. The chandeliers overhead seemed to reflect not just the brilliance of the lights but the hopes and dreams of a nation. The long mahogany table, once a barrier, had now become a bridge.

Maharaja Virendra Singh of Vindhya stood up. Tall and regal, he was the unofficial spokesman for the gathering of princes. Clearing his throat, he began, "Esteemed leaders, our forefathers have ruled their respective regions for centuries. We've seen empires rise and fall. Yet, today, we face an unprecedented crossroads. The world is changing. And if we wish to thrive, not just survive, we must change with it."

There was a pause. The magnitude of the situation filled the air.

"I propose," he continued, "that we, the princely states of India, voluntarily integrate with the Republic of India. We should become a part of this grand experiment, this mosaic of cultures, traditions, and dreams."

A murmur ran through the gathering. Then, Rani Meenakshi of Travancore rose. "I second this motion. It's time we look beyond our palace walls and see the bigger picture. It's time for unity."

One by one, the rulers voiced their support. They discussed terms, guarantees for their people, and the preservation of their unique cultural identities. But the underlying sentiment was clear: unity was the way forward.

Cyrus, touched by their decision, responded, "Your gesture will be remembered for generations. Today isn't about losing your autonomy, it's about gaining a family of millions. We will walk this path together."

As the meeting concluded, Panditji whispered to Cyrus, "This, my friend, is the beginning of a new era. One India."

Outside, the setting sun painted the sky in hues of gold and orange, a symbol of a bright future, of hopes realized, and of dreams yet to be dreamt.

As the room slowly emptied, a wave of satisfaction seemed to wash over Cyrus. The long negotiations and the palpable tension had finally led to a decision, a momentous one for the Republic of India. This was not just about merging territories, it was about forging a shared destiny.

Cyrus was engrossed in this reflection when Mr. Nair hurriedly approached him, his face pale. He whispered, "Sir, there's an urgent matter at hand."

Cyrus, alarmed by Nair's tone, asked, "What is it?"

Nair took a deep breath. "There's been a significant international incident, and its ripples have reached our shores. The imam of Ikhlaq Masjid has called for a massive protest in response to the event."

Cyrus, rubbing his temples, responded, "An international event? But why should it affect us?"

Gokhale interjected, "In our newly independent nation, the wounds are still fresh, and emotions run high. Any perceived slight or injustice to brethren overseas is taken personally. We must tread carefully."

While news of Mewad's integration brought some respite, it was short-lived. The Ikhlaq Masjid, one of the most significant religious centres in North India, posed a new challenge. The imam was a revered figure, and his words held sway among millions.

Cyrus sighed, realizing the journey ahead would demand not just political shrewdness but also a profound understanding of India's diverse heart.

He beckoned his team. "Gentlemen, we've weathered a storm today. But tomorrow brings a new challenge. Let's ensure India remains united in spirit and territory."

In his office, Cyrus contemplated his next move.

Chapter 5

CROSSROADS OF IDEOLOGY

December 1948:
The Prime Minister's Office, New Delhi

The radio played in the background, a BBC reporter narrating the world's reaction to the partitioning of the British Mandate of Palestine. Sounds of jubilation from Jewish quarters contrasted sharply with cries of anger from Arab communities. The room was thick with tension.

The years from 1947 to 1949 were tumultuous, not just for India but the entire world. The Middle East was a tinderbox, a situation set aflame by the declaration of the state of Israel. As Arab armies mobilized and crossed into the newborn state's borders, the whole world watched anxiously.

The heartbeats of New Delhi were not unaffected. In the grand courtyard of the Jama Masjid, after the evening prayers, a hush settled over the crowd.

Hamid walked in, concern evident on his face. "The creation of the Jewish state in Palestine has rattled many, Cyrus. The imam sees it as a betrayal of the Muslim world."

Cyrus responded, "We must respect international decisions, but our primary concern remains our people and our nation."

Ali Bhai added, "We need to be proactive. Let's engage the imam in dialogue."

The room was thick with tension as Gokhale opined, "A dialogue is essential, but we must also ensure that the public understands the rationale behind international decisions."

The following day, the prime minister's convoy, with its tricolour fluttering, reached Ikhlaq Masjid. The mosque, a magnificent structure with towering minarets, was surrounded by thousands of protestors.

Inside, the imam, an elderly man with a flowing white beard, received Cyrus and his delegation.

"Prime Minister," the imam began, his voice strong and echoing throughout the chamber, "the Muslim world feels betrayed. How do you justify supporting the creation of a Jewish state on Palestinian land? The Muslim community in India is deeply troubled by the ongoing conflict in Palestine. We've already felt betrayed once, when the dream of a new homeland was promised but not realized. Our hopes were dashed, our trust broken."

The imam continued, "Now, as our brethren in Palestine face turmoil and strife, India cannot remain silent or neutral. We must take a clear stand, show our support. If necessary, we should be prepared to send soldiers and aid to assist Palestine. The Muslim community in India cannot endure another betrayal."

Cyrus, taking a deep breath, replied, "Respected Imam, India respects the rights of all nations and their people. We have no direct influence over international decisions. Our primary goal is the peace and progress of our nation. We need unity, not division."

The imam, his face impassive, responded, "And what of the rights of the Palestinians?"

Patel Sahib interjected, "The situation in Palestine is complex. While we empathize with the Palestinian cause, our stance is for a peaceful resolution. We cannot let international affairs dictate our national harmony."

The conversation went on for hours. Outside, the crowd grew restless. Chants, slogans, and songs filled the air. The media had gathered, making it a spectacle for the nation.

As the evening descended, Cyrus emerged from the mosque with the imam beside him. They addressed the crowd together.

"We have reached an understanding," Cyrus began. "India stands for peace. Our decisions will always prioritize our national interest, but we will always advocate for justice on the international stage."

The imam nodded. "We may not always agree, but dialogue is essential. Let's not allow external issues to divide our great nation."

The crowd, witnessing this unexpected alliance, dispersed peacefully.

Later, in a quiet, oak-panelled room in Delhi, the advisory committee debated the situation. Ali Bhai and Hamid, deeply concerned, expressed their thoughts. "India must declare its support for the Arab world," Ali Bhai insisted.

"Not only is it the right thing to do, but it will also resonate with a large part of our populace," added Hamid.

Cyrus, his gaze fixed on the world map, took a moment before he responded. "I understand the sentiments, gentlemen. But we need to think of a solution that brings everyone to the table and is in line with our new ethos."

Hamid, exasperated, said, "Cyrus, this isn't a philosophical debate. It's real lives and our responsibility."

Cyrus responded, his tone measured, "It's not about choosing sides. It's about understanding the human story. We cannot forget the years of prejudice and immense suffering the Jewish community has faced."

Hamid, running his fingers through his beard, said, "But our immediate concern should be our brothers and sisters in the Arab nations."

Cyrus turned to face Hamid squarely and said, "Yes, and I hear you. But India's vision should be to bring unity, not deepen divisions. We must use our influence, our moral standing, to broker peace, not take sides."

"You talk of the Jewish plight," Hamid retorted sharply, "but what about the Palestinians who are now losing their homes?"

"You speak of unity and understanding, Cyrus," began Ali Bhai, his voice resonating with conviction. "Yet, in our own history, we've supported the Muslim brothers during the Khilafat Movement. Where was this doctrine of neutrality then?"

Cyrus, showing no signs of backing down, responded, "Ali Bhai, the Khilafat Movement was a response to an imperialistic move. It was a stand against oppression. But now, we are in a different era. Brotherhood should not be confined by religion. It should encompass humanity."

"You can't ignore the bond of faith," Ali Bhai countered.

"Nor can you ignore the Holocaust," Cyrus shot back, his gaze piercing. "If there's any community that has been systematically persecuted, marginalized, and pushed to the edge of existence, it's the Jews. If there's any community that needs brotherhood, a sense of national identity, it's them."

Ali Bhai sighed deeply, the consequences of history and the pressures of the present pressing down on him. "I understand the Jews have suffered," he said, "but we have a responsibility to our Muslim brethren, too."

Cyrus nodded, appreciating Ali Bhai's concern. "Our responsibility is to humanity, Ali Bhai. To broker peace. To ensure that history doesn't repeat itself. To ensure that no community, be it Jewish, Muslim, Hindu, or any other, suffers the way they did."

As the sun set over the prime minister's residence, casting long shadows on the plush carpets, the room was tense with anticipation. Each leader present held a perspective, every argument stemming from their individual understanding of the nation's interests and their personal ideologies.

In the midst of a heated discussion among the key figures of the government, an unexpected interruption came in the form of Mr. Nair. He entered the room with an unusual haste, his usually composed demeanour replaced by a sense of pressing urgency.

"Excuse me for the intrusion," Nair began, his voice cutting through the thick air of deliberation that hung in the room. The seriousness was evident as all eyes turned towards him, a silent acknowledgement of the rarity of such interruptions.

In his hand, he clutched a copy of the evening edition of the *Times of India*, its headline screaming for attention. Without a word, he unfolded the paper and laid it on the table where the leaders were gathered. The headline was bold and unequivocal, announcing that the United States had decided to send its 7th Fleet to the Sinai Peninsula.

The room fell into a momentary silence as the implications of this development began to sink in. The presence of the US fleet in such a strategically critical region signified a substantial escalation in the international response to the ongoing crisis.

Cyrus leaned forward, his eyes scanning the article, each word adding a layer of complexity to the already intricate geopolitical puzzle. Panditji's brow furrowed in deep thought, Patel Sahib's lips pressed into a thin line, and Ali Bhai's gaze remained fixed on the newspaper, reflective of the weighty considerations now placed before them. The meeting, initially focused on the bilateral concerns of Palestine and Israel, had suddenly been thrust into the broader context of global politics and its unpredictable dynamics.

"This changes things." Cyrus finally spoke, his voice steady yet laden with the newfound implications of this revelation. "The involvement of the US in this manner could shift the balance in the region. We need to reassess our position and response immediately."

Nair interjected. "Sir, might I suggest speaking with the US president? The Americans hold significant influence in this matter." His statement was accompanied by his signature grin, which seemed out of place given the seriousness of the matter.

Panditji adjusted his glasses. "Nair has a point. But Cyrus, the United Nations was created for such conflicts. We should push for an international consensus and mediate for peace."

Patel Sahib scoffed. "Consensus? These are grave times! We need action, not mere words. Israel has always been supportive of our cause. We must stand by them now."

Cyrus looked around the room, his piercing eyes meeting each gaze, the significance of the decision ahead pressing heavily on his shoulders. *The last thing we need right now,* Cyrus thought, *is for US naval power to start influencing the dynamics in the Arabian Peninsula as well. But I think I may have to speak to the president of the United States sooner if not later.*

With a deep sigh, he finally broke the silence. "Gentlemen, each one of you offers a path, each valuable in its own way. But we must act keeping in mind the legacy we want to leave behind."

Cyrus stood, his hands resting firmly on the table. "The burden of our choices will echo through the annals of history. This is not just about a war in the Middle East but a testament to India's character on the world stage."

He paused, his gaze shifting from one face to another, absorbing the weight of the collective anticipation. "I need time to reflect," he declared softly but with an undertone of authority.

"Hamid," he said, turning to his confidant, "meet the imam. Assure him, and through him our countrymen, that we shall approach this with wisdom and fairness. We seek harmony, not only on our soil but everywhere. We've faced riots and challenges that have torn at the fabric of our society. Our decisions now must ensure that the tapestry of our nation remains strong and united."

The room, which had been abuzz with passionate discourse moments earlier, was now cloaked in thoughtful silence. Each leader felt the magnitude of Cyrus's words, understanding that the decisions made in these rooms would shape the destinies of millions.

Hamid nodded. "I'll see to it right away."

Cyrus gave a brief nod of acknowledgement. "Gentlemen, I thank you for your counsel. But now, I must reflect in solitude." Without another word, he turned, slowly walking towards his bedroom. The heavy wooden door closed behind him, serving as a barrier between the raging storm of geopolitical strategy and the solitude of his introspective chamber.

The controversy over the Israel-Palestinian issue still lingered in the corridors of Parliament, but for Prime Minister Engineer, a new domestic challenge was brewing. The heart of the matter lay in the bustling city of Dhaka.

January 1949: Dhaka, East India

Dhaka, a city built on the banks of the Buriganga and known for its vibrant culture and historical significance, had grown into a major industrial hub over the past few decades. At its centre stood the Dhaka Cotton Textile Mills, a symbol of India's industrial prowess and its evolving landscape. However, the city's progress came with its share of issues.

The sun bore down on the city of Dhakka, and its intensity was matched by the fury of the thousands gathered outside the colossal gates of the Dhakka Cotton Textile Mills. The usually cacophonous looms inside were silent, but the chants outside resonated with an urgency that was impossible to ignore.

"Fair pay! Fair pay!" the crowd roared in unison, their voices echoing across the landscape.

Banners and signs painted in bold reds and blacks floated above the sea of people with slogans such as 'Workers are not Slaves' and 'We Demand Our Due'. Men and women, their clothes stained with the white fluff of cotton and sweat, stood shoulder to shoulder, united in their cause. They had been the backbone of the mill, some having dedicated their entire lives to it, and the dwindling pay coupled with rising living costs had pushed them to the brink.

In the midst of the crowd stood Ravi, a young and fervent union leader with a fiery spirit. He climbed atop an improvised podium—a wooden cart borrowed from a nearby vendor—and raised his hand for silence.

"We have toiled day and night," Ravi began, his voice echoing powerfully. "We have turned this mill into one of the most profitable ventures in Dhaka, and what do we get in return? Pennies! While the owners sit in their lavish mansions, we struggle to feed our families."

The crowd erupted in agreement, their anger palpable. Mothers held up their malnourished children, a grim testament to their plight.

Suddenly, a sleek black car, noticeably out of place amidst the surroundings, made its way hesitantly through the outskirts of the crowd. The crowd's attention turned, and a hush fell upon them. The door opened, and out stepped a tall, well-dressed man, recognized by many as Mr. Das, the owner of the mills.

He cleared his throat. "I understand your concerns," he began, his voice quivering slightly under the weight of thousands of eyes upon him. "I promise to revisit the wages."

Ravi, quick to respond, jumped off the cart and approached him. "Revisit? When, sir? In another decade? We want assurance. We need a written agreement. No more hollow promises!"

Mr. Das seemed taken aback by the direct confrontation. "I… I promise to convene a meeting with the union leaders by tomorrow. We'll discuss and draft a new wage agreement."

The crowd, sensing a small victory, erupted into cheers. Ravi, however, maintained a stern face. "Remember, Mr. Das," he pointed at the vast sea of workers behind him, "this is our strength. We trust you'll make the right decision, or this," he motioned towards the silent mill, "stays silent."

The rising sun of 1949 had barely begun to dispel the lingering shadows of colonialism when a fresh challenge began to foment in the industrial heartlands of India. The distant tremors from Dhakka's cotton mills soon vibrated across the nation's varied industrial zones.

Coal miners in Dhanbad left their pits. Ludhiana's metal workers laid down their tools. Everywhere, the labour force was uniting in a chorus of demand and dissent. As days turned into weeks, this wasn't just about Dhaka anymore; it was about the broader struggle of India's working class.

Fuelled by international influences and the successes of the USSR, a significant segment of the workforce began clamouring for a shift to a socialist model. Streets that had once echoed with cries for independence from the British now rang with shouts of "Inquilab Zindabad!" and "Workers of the world, unite!"

In the prime minister's office, the stress of this escalating situation was palpable. Prime Minister Engineer, in the embryonic stages of India's republic, now confronted a dilemma that could shape the future trajectory of the nation.

Hints of a socialist allure, with its promise of egalitarianism and rights for workers, now contrasted sharply against India's original vision of a mixed economy. A delegation led by members of the Communist Party of India marched to the PM's office, advocating for a pivot in India's economic doctrine.

Mr. Nair, with a twinkle in his eye, remarked, "Mr. Prime Minister, the breeze from the Russian tundra seems to be chilling our workers, too!"

Cyrus, offering a weary smile in response, gathered his cabinet for an urgent discussion. The room was thick with debate.

"We need to take control of this situation," Patel Sahib's voice boomed. "This isn't just about wages anymore; it's about the very soul of our nation."

Ali Bhai countered, "These workers have valid grievances. The USSR's progress is noteworthy. Maybe we need to reconsider our stance."

Amidst the cacophony, Panditji calmly interjected, "It's not about suppression or imitation. It's about listening and understanding. Our strength has always been in our adaptability."

After reflecting upon the discourse, Cyrus finally said, "We can't forsake our foundational vision. But we must heed our workers' voices. It's time for open dialogue—with union leaders, workers, and industry stalwarts alike."

Thus, a decision crystallized. The government would initiate a series of nationwide dialogues to mediate between labourers, industry magnates, and policymakers. Their objective: to formulate a renewed industrial covenant for India, one that would merge aspiration with reality, progress with fairness. The journey would be challenging, but the intention was clear—a united way forward for the fledgling republic.

Questions were raised in rallies. Was the government doing enough to protect the rights of the workers? Would Dhaka be the starting point of a national movement?

Prime Minister Engineer knew the importance of addressing this issue head-on. He convened an emergency meeting with his core team, including Panditji, Mr. Nair, and other key ministers.

The mood in the prime minister's office was sombre. Maps of industrial regions lay sprawled across the large mahogany table, marked with red flags indicating areas of unrest. Advisors bustled around, deep in conversations, devising plans to quell the growing storm.

Cyrus, leaning over the table, traced a line from Dhaka to the eastern industrial belt. "Perhaps I should visit each of these sectors," he mused aloud, "meet with the workers and their leaders, understand their grievances first-hand."

Before any of the advisors could react, a familiar chirpy voice piped up from the doorway. Mr. Nair, holding a cup of his favourite South Indian filter coffee, walked in with his characteristic confident swagger.

"Mr. Prime Minister," he began, taking a careful sip of his coffee, "with all due respect, while your hands-on approach is commendable, this isn't the time for field trips."

Cyrus turned to him, slightly taken aback by the bluntness. "Mr. Nair, the nation is on the brink. I need to be with the people."

Mr. Nair adjusted his round spectacles and replied, "Indeed, sir, but you need to be with all the people. Visiting these sectors will not bring the immediate calm we need. And quite frankly, you're the prime minister, not an intern doing groundwork."

A few advisors stifled their chuckles, well accustomed to Mr. Nair's blend of humour and wisdom.

"Address the nation," Nair continued, his tone more earnest now. "Speak from the heart. Let them know where India stands, what you envision for this great nation. Lead as the leader you are."

Cyrus looked into the distance, weighing Nair's words. After a few moments, he nodded. "Arrange a radio address for this evening."

Mr. Nair beamed. "Will do, sir! And might I suggest a touch of South Indian filter coffee before the address? Works wonders for the nerves!"

With a chuckle, Cyrus replied, "I might just take you up on that."

The evening grew darker, setting the stage for a radio address that would echo through the ages. Homes, offices, teashops, and even bustling bazaars turned silent as people gathered around their radio sets to hear their prime minister's voice.

The room was alive with activity—the teletype machines rattling away, radios humming the latest news updates, and phones constantly ringing.

Mrs. Chatterjee, amidst the organized chaos, was busy jotting down notes, her saree perfectly draped and not a hair out of place.

Nair sauntered in, adjusting his round glasses, with Cyrus following him closely. "Ah, Mrs. Chatterjee," Nair began, a playful tone in his voice, "I hear the newspapermen have coined a new title for you—'The Silent Guardian of PMO'. A bit dramatic, don't you think?"

Mrs. Chatterjee's eyes met his, unflinching. "Coming from the man who's called 'The Whisperer of the Corridors', I'll take that as a compliment."

Cyrus, sensing the charged atmosphere, quickly intervened, "Let's keep our wit for the journalists, shall we? We've got the prime minister's address in an hour, and we can't afford any hiccups."

Not missing a chance to rib Mrs. Chatterjee, Nair commented, "Indeed! And with Mrs. Chatterjee's legendary efficiency, I'm sure all is in order."

Mrs. Chatterjee gave a tight smile. "Indeed, Mr. Nair. If only everyone held themselves to such standards, our jobs would be a tad easier."

Cyrus sighed, trying to steer the conversation back. "Let's focus. We're in the cradle of a new India. Let's not forget that."

The soft hum of the radio studio equipment filled the room as Cyrus prepared to address the nation. The microphone in front of him seemed to await his speech, a conduit to the millions who would be hanging on to his every word.

"My dear fellow countrymen," Cyrus began, his voice carrying the weight of his responsibility, "in the wake of recent events, with voices calling for change and a look towards the East, I come before you tonight to discuss the path India shall tread."

Clearing his throat, he continued, "India stands at a crossroads. To our west, we see the allure of capitalism, to our east, the promise of communism. Both have their merits, and both, their flaws. But tonight, I must make our stance clear."

There was a pause, a deep intake of breath, and Cyrus's voice rang out assertively, "India will remain a capitalistic nation."

A silent gasp swept through homes as millions listened in rapt attention.

He continued, "I, as a political science student, have studied both models. While capitalism has its evils, the darkness it casts does not overshadow the potential it holds. Communism, as noble as its ideals may be, demands a rigidity and uniformity that our diverse nation cannot, and should not, adhere to."

The conviction in his voice was palpable. "I predict that in the decades to come, the world will see communism's inherent flaws. It will witness the collapse of a system that believes in strict equality but not in the beauty of individual spirit and enterprise. I believe not in equality but in equity—where each individual has the tools and opportunities tailored to their needs and aspirations."

The silence was piercing. The nation hung on to every word.

"And so," Cyrus proclaimed, "while we embrace capitalism, we shall also safeguard our people against its excesses. I am announcing the creation of a Ministry of Social Justice to ensure every individual, every worker, has their rights protected and their voices heard."

He concluded, "Furthermore, stringent industrial laws will be enacted to balance the scales of power. Industries will flourish but not at the expense of our workers. We shall strive to ensure that prosperity is achieved, not just for a few, but for all."

As the radio waves fell silent, there was a hushed awe. The address was a masterstroke, deftly walking the tightrope of economics and emotions. Mr. Nair, observing from a corner, couldn't help but quip, "Mr. Prime Minister, you've truly got a capital idea there!"

And so, as the sun set over the Parliament building, a new chapter in the story of Dhaka began to unfold. One that would test the mettle of Cyrus's leadership and the resilience of Indian democracy

The next morning, the sun had barely risen, and the corridors of the prime minister's office were abuzz. Patel Sahib, a towering presence and a crucial pillar of Cyrus's government, strode purposefully into the prime minister's chambers.

"Cyrus! Your radio address, while eloquent, has created ripples we hadn't anticipated. The union leaders are in an uproar. They see it as a declaration against their interests."

Cyrus looked up, rubbing his temples. "I just wanted to give clarity, Patel Sahib. The ambiguity was leading to unrest."

Patel Sahib leaned on the table. "And clarity is important. But you must remember, Cyrus, it's not just what you say, but how it's perceived. You've laid out our economic vision on a national platform. Now, it's time to make the key players part of this journey."

Cyrus looked puzzled. "How do you suggest we do that?"

"A personal touch, my boy. Invite the union leaders to lunch at your residence. Let them see you're as invested in their concerns as they are. Talk, listen, negotiate."

Cyrus pondered over the idea. "Lunch, you say? A chance to talk beyond the formalities of the office?"

Patel Sahib smiled. "Exactly. A place where barriers come down and understanding can be fostered."

On the day of the lunch, the sun was high, casting a warm glow over the expansive lawns of the prime minister's residence. White canopies had been set up, under which elegantly laid tables awaited their guests. The fragrance of roses from the garden mixed with the inviting aromas of a sumptuous spread that was being laid out.

As the union leaders began to arrive, they looked around with a mixture of curiosity and caution. For many, it was their first time in such opulent surroundings, and while the ambience was inviting, they were well aware of the political undercurrents.

Cyrus stepped out, greeting each leader personally. His affable demeanour, genuine warmth, and firm handshake set many at ease. They took their seats, and lively chatter filled the air, punctuated by Mr. Nair's occasional jests that sent ripples of laughter around.

Once everyone had settled, Cyrus began, "Thank you all for coming. I believe in open dialogue, and today, I hope we can talk as representatives of this nation, not as adversaries."

Raghav Desai, a formidable union leader from Dhaka leaned forward. "Mr. Prime Minister, our workers are restless. They hear tales of the riches of capitalism but only see the widening gap between the haves and the have-nots."

Cyrus nodded, taking a moment to frame his thoughts. "I understand your concerns, Raghav. Capitalism, if unchecked, can lead to disparities. But it also fosters innovation, encourages competition, and most importantly, offers individual freedoms. Our job is to strike a balance. While we embrace capitalism, we must also ensure regulations that prevent its excesses."

"But, sir," intervened Geeta Malik, another influential leader, "we've seen how the West operates. Wealth accumulates at the top while the workers remain exploited."

Cyrus acknowledged her point. "Which is why, Geeta, we're not blindly adopting Western capitalism. Our approach will be rooted in Indian values—where the community matters, where businesses don't just chase profits but also have a responsibility towards their employees and society."

Mr. Nair chimed in with a grin, "Think of it like our Indian curries. We take the best spices from everywhere, but the final dish is uniquely ours."

There was light laughter, but Raghav persisted, "And how do we ensure this balance?"

Cyrus smiled. "By creating stringent industrial laws, ensuring workers' rights, and most crucially, by keeping channels of communication open. Today's lunch isn't a one-off event. I envision regular interactions, debates, and discussions. Together, we will shape this nation's industrial future."

The lively chatter was momentarily silenced by the soft chime of a clock, indicating the start of a new hour. As the union leaders sipped on their drinks, awaiting dessert, Cyrus stood up, motioning for attention.

"I'd like to make an announcement," he began, his voice betraying the solemnity of the occasion.

The gathering leaned in, curiosity evident.

"After much thought and deliberation, I've decided to appoint Dr. Alluwalia as the special economic advisor to the prime minister."

A murmur ran through the group. Dr. Alluwalia, while revered in academic circles, had always maintained a respectful distance from the political limelight.

Cyrus continued, "A PhD from Oxford and a master's from Cambridge, his academic prowess is commendable. But what impresses me most is his vision for India and its alignment with our ideals. He's going to be our compass, guiding us through the complexities of laying out a financial roadmap for our fledgling nation."

A side door opened, and in walked a robust figure. A distinguished-looking sardar with a flowing beard, Dr. Alluwalia's bright blue turban was a stark contrast to the muted colours of the room. His face, framed by the beard and thick glasses, radiated intelligence. And yet, instead of the aloofness one might expect from someone of his stature, his eyes twinkled with genuine warmth.

As he approached the head of the table, Cyrus introduced him with a sense of pride. "Ladies and gentlemen, meet Dr. Alluwalia."

The leaders, already at ease from the lunch, exchanged hopeful glances. Here was a man who, by the very virtue of his genial nature, seemed open to understanding and addressing their concerns. Dr. Alluwalia, sensing the atmosphere, began with gratitude.

"I'm honoured to serve our nation in this role. My roots might be deep in academia, but my heart and soul are with the people of this nation. I promise to work hand in hand with all of you for our collective betterment."

Mr. Nair, added, "And I'm just glad we have someone who can explain the economy in terms I might actually understand!" The room erupted in laughter, the final remnants of any lingering tension dissolving.

Watching the camaraderie develop before his eyes, Cyrus felt a surge of hope. The journey ahead, he knew, would be challenging, but with allies like these, he felt ready to face whatever lay ahead.

Chapter 6

DISCORD IN UNITY

April 1949: The Prime Minister's Office

The early April sun was unusually scorching for New Delhi as a young messenger scurried through the sprawling corridors of the prime minister's office. The envelope he carried bore the seal of the national emblem, a symbol of urgency. As he handed it to Mr. Nair, his face was tense with the significance of its contents.

Inside the ornate office, large curtains billowed gently with the afternoon breeze. The room was filled with the muffled sounds of the city preparing for the evening. Cyrus sat behind his large wooden desk, engrossed in files and dispatches from various parts of the country. Noticing Mr. Nair's entrance, he looked up, a welcoming smile on his face. "Ah, Nair! What brings you here with such a serious expression?"

Mr. Nair cleared his throat, adjusting his glasses. "Sir, there's a situation in Sindh that requires immediate attention. The president of the Sindh Bhasha Sangh, a revered figure in the region, has announced a fast unto death. His demand? Recognition of Modokoni as the official language of the state."

Cyrus leaned back, absorbing the gravity of the situation. "This is unexpected. We've been promoting linguistic diversity, but a fast unto death is a serious measure. What's the public sentiment?"

Nair hesitated, choosing his words carefully. "The public seems divided, but a significant portion supports the Sangh's stance. Local newspapers have taken up the issue with fervour, and there are reports of protests in Sindh's major cities."

Cyrus rubbed his temples, the task of governance pressing down. "Language… It's the soul of culture. But we also need to think about national unity and practicality. We need a balanced approach."

Mr. Nair nodded. "I concur, sir. We must tread cautiously. The linguistic sentiment runs deep."

Cyrus sat at his desk, hands steepled, deep in thought. News had just reached him of escalating tensions in Sindh. Protests had erupted, with clashes between linguistic groups threatening to tear apart the fabric of unity he so earnestly hoped to weave. There were reports of agitated mobs and demands for statehood based on language. He knew he had to act quickly.

Turning to his trusted aide, Nair, he said, "Summon S.K. Banerjee for me. I believe he's the man for what's next."

Within the hour, Banerjee, a seasoned civil servant with a reputation for thoroughness and an in-depth understanding of India's complex socio-political tapestry, stood before him.

"Cyrusji," Banerjee began, but Cyrus raised a hand to halt him.

"Banerjee," Cyrus said, looking him directly in the eyes, "I need you to form a committee. A committee that will delve deep into the complexities of our land and recommend a just and effective organization of our states."

Banerjee blinked, taken aback. "But, sir, I thought the decision was already made?"

"It was," Cyrus admitted, "But Sindh is a warning. We must tread carefully. We need a report that examines the feasibility of our decision, the potential pitfalls, and most importantly, how to ensure the unity of our diverse nation."

Banerjee nodded slowly, processing the magnitude of the responsibility. "I understand, sir. We'll need experts, linguists, historians, sociologists—"

"And representatives from every region," Cyrus added. "This report should not be the voice of a few but the collective wisdom of our nation."

"I will ensure it, Mr. Prime Minister," Banerjee assured him.

As Banerjee left the room, Cyrus felt a sense of relief wash over him. He had taken the first step to ensure that the reorganization of states would not be a hasty decision but one rooted in research, dialogue, and inclusivity.

In Sindh, the streets bore the marks of recent violence. Burnt shops, homes vandalized, and the fear palpable. A large crowd had gathered outside the district court, chanting slogans. Aisha, a teacher, shouted to her friend over the din, "Language is our identity, our heritage. Can Delhi understand that?"

Her friend, Priya, from a linguistic minority, replied, "But must we spill blood for it?"

As the sun began its descent, casting long shadows over the landscape of Sindh, Cyrus and Gokhale arrived in the troubled state for a meeting with Raja Krishnan, an influential monarch and patron of the Sindh Bhasha Sangh. The palace was inscribed with symbols of the Modokoni language, indicative of the raja's deep-rooted linguistic pride.

"Prime Minister," began Raja Krishnan, offering Cyrus a seat, "you can't expect to curb our linguistic pride with administrative mandates."

Cyrus, choosing his words carefully, replied, "It isn't about curbing pride, Maharaja. It's about fostering unity. The essence of language is communication, understanding. Isn't it ironic if it becomes a source of division?"

"But you cannot ignore our history and identity. Modokoni isn't just a language; it's the heartbeat of Sindh."

After the crucial meeting with Raja Krishnan, Cyrus turned to Gokhale. "Gokhale, I need you to stay here in Sindh," he said, his voice firm yet underscored with a sense of urgency. "We need to engage with the local leaders, understand their concerns deeply, and address them effectively. There's no one else I trust more to navigate this situation."

Gokhale nodded, understanding the seriousness of the task ahead. He was well aware of the delicate nature of the crisis, where every conversation, every gesture carried weight. "I'll do everything in my capacity to bring stability," he assured Cyrus. "It's vital that we bring the leaders into confidence, to show them that their voices are heard and respected at the highest levels."

Cyrus clasped Gokhale's shoulder in a gesture of solidarity. "Your presence here will be reassuring to them. Your ability to listen and negotiate is what Sindh needs right now."

As Cyrus prepared to leave Sindh, he and Gokhale exchanged a look of mutual understanding. This was more than a political mission; it was about the integrity of the nation and the delicate balance of respecting cultural diversity while maintaining national unity.

Gokhale spent the following days meeting with local leaders, community heads, and influential figures in Sindh. His approach was one of empathy and respect, seeking to build bridges and find common ground. His discussions were marked by a genuine desire to understand the heart of Sindh's concerns and to relay these faithfully back to the central government for a comprehensive and inclusive solution. Gokhale assured them, "The prime minister's intention is to create a harmonious environment. He believes that segregating based on language will lead to further divisions."

Meanwhile, Cyrus, back in the capital, awaited Gokhale's updates, confident in his abilities but aware of the complex nature of the situation. The resolution of the Sindh issue would be a critical turning point, not just for the state but for the entire nation, as it grappled with the challenges of balancing regional aspirations with national unity.

In a café across town, journalists were buzzing. Sneha, a reporter from Delhi, was having coffee with Rajan, a local correspondent.

"Cyrus has stirred a hornet's nest," Rajan remarked, sipping his coffee.

Sneha replied, "Maybe, but isn't it necessary? Today it's language, tomorrow it could be dialect, then maybe folklore. Where does it end?"

In another corner of Sindh, Aisha and Priya were spearheading a community initiative, teaching children of both linguistic backgrounds. They believed education could bridge divides. Their school was a symbol of hope, a testament that unity could prevail.

A week later, a grand assembly was organized in Sindh's main square. The event was pitched as a cultural exchange, where both Modokoni and minority linguistic groups showcased their heritage. Music, dance, poetry readings, and plays filled the square.

However, despite these initiatives, sporadic violence continued. The voices of dissent grew stronger. The leaders of the Sindh Bhasha Sangh organized a massive rally, drawing thousands. Raja Krishnan, in a fiery speech, declared, "We will not let our language be relegated to the pages of history."

In the midst of escalating tensions in Sindh, Gokhale's patience was beginning to fray. The atmosphere of unrest and violence in the state was a growing concern, and he felt an urgency to bring the situation under control. Picking up the phone, he dialled Cyrus, his tone reflecting his unease.

"Cyrus, the situation here is deteriorating. We need to act fast." Gokhale's voice crackled over the line, marked by an uncharacteristic edge of impatience. "Every day we delay, the unrest grows. We need a resolution, and we need it now."

On the other end of the line, in the calm confines of his office, Cyrus listened intently, understanding the exigency but also aware of the complexities involved. "I hear your concerns, Gokhale," Cyrus replied, his voice steady, "but we need a little more time. The Banerjee committee's report will be pivotal in shaping our long-term strategy for Sindh. It's crucial we get this right."

There was a pause as Gokhale absorbed Cyrus's words, the sound of distant protests echoing faintly in the background of his call. "We might not have the luxury of time, Cyrus. People are getting restless."

Cyrus, thoughtful for a moment, then offered a temporary solution. "Okay. For the time being, propose a two-language policy to Raja Krishnan. Assure him that both the local language and the minority language will be given equal importance in administrative and educational spheres. It might help to ease some of the tension."

Gokhale listened, the suggestion offering a glimmer of hope in the prevailing uncertainty. "I'll discuss it with Raja Krishnan today," he responded, a renewed sense of purpose in his voice. "It could be the conciliatory gesture we need to calm the waters until the committee's recommendations are ready."

The conversation ended with Gokhale feeling slightly more hopeful. He knew the road ahead was fraught with challenges, but Cyrus's steady leadership and the potential interim solution offered a ray of hope. As he prepared to meet with Raja Krishnan, Gokhale felt a renewed determination to steer Sindh towards a peaceful resolution, one step at a time.

Gokhale invited Raja Krishnan and representatives of the linguistic minorities for a closed-door meeting.

Emerging from the meeting, a joint statement was released. Till the findings of the Banerjee Committee were out, Sindh would introduce a dual-language policy in public domains, giving equal importance to Modokoni and the significant minority language.

In Delhi, Cyrus was under immense pressure. Protests demanding linguistic states erupted nationwide. "We must listen to the people," Hamid, still seething from the Palestine issue, argued in a cabinet meeting. Patel Sahib, on the other hand, was in favour of strategic state division. The nation held its breath.

Two Months Later

Cyrus was deep in thought, pondering the implications of linguistic divisions, when Mr. Nair strolled in. "Mr. Prime Minister, have you ever tried speaking Tamil? It's like doing yoga with your tongue!"

Cyrus laughed. "No, Nair, I haven't, but now you've piqued my interest."

The evening sun cast a mellow orange hue over the majestic prime minister's residence. Within the ornate drawing room, a large teakwood table lay covered with files, charts, and maps. At its head, Cyrus waited with bated breath, surrounded by key members of his cabinet as they waited for a crucial meeting on S.K. Banerjee's report.

The gentle chime of the doorbell announced the arrival of S.K. Banerjee. He was ushered in, holding a thick file embossed with the Ashoka emblem. His face, usually calm and composed, bore signs of fatigue, but his eyes sparkled with the confidence of someone who'd completed a herculean task.

"Good evening, Prime Minister, ministers," Banerjee greeted, offering a slight bow.

Cyrus rose, extending a hand. "Banerjee, I trust you've had some sleep in the past two months?" he quipped, trying to lighten the mood.

Banerjee smiled. "A few winks here and there, sir."

Patel Sahib chimed in, "We've been eagerly awaiting this report, Banerjee. The whole nation has."

Gokhale added, "We hope it provides the path forward."

Banerjee nodded. "With all humility, I believe it does. My team and I met leaders, representatives, saints, and seers from every nook and corner of the country. We listened, argued, and at times, pacified. The report reflects the voice of India."

Cyrus gestured to the table. "Please, share your findings."

The magnificent room in the prime minister's residence was tense. Leaders from various factions and regions sat silently, observing the grand map of India sprawled across the table. The map, detailing every nook and corner of the nation, was marked with bright-coloured boundaries, clearly demarcating the new divisions.

The room was heavy with anticipation. The grand map and files lined the grand oak table, evidence of the numerous discussions that had been taking place for the past weeks. The cabinet members were deep in discussion, leaning into one another, murmuring opinions, and debating options.

Finally, the report was ready. Banerjee, with his calm demeanour, presented. "Given the sentiments and administrative efficiency, it's advised to have sixteen linguistic states."

Banerjee was adamant. "Linguistic states, Cyrus. It's the only way forward. We need to respect the cultural and linguistic identities of our diverse populace. Only then will India find its true identity."

Cyrus listened intently, his fingers drumming rhythmically on the table, absorbing the perspectives and arguments laid before him. However, he seemed distant, lost in his thoughts. He remembered his father's gentle voice, echoing words of wisdom and hope, "India belongs to everyone. It is a saviour for those without a home, a shelter for the shelterless."

The room grew silent as all eyes turned to Cyrus, waiting for a verdict, a decision that would shape the future of the nation.

Taking a deep breath, Cyrus rose from his chair, his gaze unwavering. "I have heard everyone's arguments, and I appreciate the depth of thought and emotion each one of you has put into this. But there is something more to India than just language. There's an underlying unity, a binding force."

Clearly understanding the significance of his next declaration, he began, "Ladies and gentlemen, we are a vast and diverse nation, both in terms of culture and geography. However, to ensure smooth administration and governance, we've decided on a geographical division rather than a linguistic one."

He pointed to the map. "These are the new states of our Republic."

1. **Northwest:** Stretching from the historic city of Peshawar, covering the sands of Rajasthan, and reaching up to the snow-covered peaks of Kashmir.

2. **Northern Region:** Starting from the cold terrains of Leh, encompassing the vast plains and ending at the cultural heartland of Bihar.

3. **Northeast:** A blend of Orissa, the vibrant Bengal, the bustling city of Dhaka, and the pristine northeastern states.

4. **Western Region:** The dynamic state of Bombay, the regal territories of Saurashtra and Junagarh, inclusive of the ports of Karachi and Sindh.

5. **Central Region:** A combination of the erstwhile princely state of Bhopal, the vibrant Vidharbha region of Nagpur, and the historic city of Jhansi.

6. **Southern Region:** From the cultural hub of Madras, extending to the Nizam's Hyderabad, covering the coastal kingdom of Malabar and the historic Deccan region.

A murmur went through the room, each leader contemplating the implications of these new divisions. Some felt the division was strategic and would lead to better governance. Others were concerned about the regional identities being submerged.

Panditji cleared his throat. "Cyrus, this is a bold move. Our country's diverse linguistics are its essence. Are you certain this will not dilute our rich cultural heritage?"

Cyrus nodded. "I understand your concerns, Panditji. However, our aim is unity, administrative efficiency, and holistic development. By dividing on a geographical basis, we intend to ensure that no linguistic or cultural group feels dominant or marginalized."

Cyrus leaned back in his leather-bound chair, a deep sigh escaping him as the significance of the decision he had just made seemed to momentarily press upon the room. His fingers brushed over the papers that held the future of a nation's identity, his eyes then shifting to Mrs. Chatterjee, who stood with an attentive poise.

"Mrs. Chatterjee," he began, his voice steady with the authority of his office, "the announcement must go out without delay. The people of India deserve to know of our commitment to both unity and respect for diversity."

Mrs. Chatterjee, ever the picture of efficiency, nodded promptly, her pen poised above her notepad. "It shall be done, sir," she affirmed. "I will have the press release prepared within the hour and sent to the *Times of India* for inclusion in tomorrow's morning edition."

Cyrus observed her with a mixture of gratitude and urgency. "Ensure it captures the essence of our intention," he said, a firm undertone to his words. "This is not merely administrative restructuring; it is the acknowledgement of the cultural and linguistic plurality of our nation."

Mrs. Chatterjee understood the importance encapsulated in those lines. "It will be conveyed with the utmost clarity and precision, sir. The nation will see your vision as one that respects the very fabric of our society," she replied confidently.

Satisfied, Cyrus gave a curt nod. "Good. Have the draft sent to me for final approval before it goes out. And Mrs. Chatterjee," he added, his gaze locking with hers, "this is to be expedited. The first rays of tomorrow's sun should carry the news to every corner of our land."

"Absolutely, sir. You will have it on your desk within the hour for your signature," she assured him, before turning to briskly exit the room, her saree swishing silently as she moved.

Cyrus turned his gaze out of the window, where the bustling streets of the capital lay. He could almost hear the heartbeat of the country, each throb a myriad of voices waiting to be heard. Tomorrow, they would know that their leader had not only heard them but had dared to act in the preservation of their identity.

The room continued to buzz with discussions, disagreements, and debates, but the decision had been made. As the sun set on Delhi, the horizon of a new India was just beginning to rise.

Two Days after the Announcement

In the aftermath of Cyrus's pivotal announcement delineating states on linguistic lines, the atmosphere in the PMO was one of quiet anticipation. The usual clatter of typewriters and shuffle of papers seemed to pause as Mr. Nair pondered over the decision that had just been made public. The consequences of its implications were not lost on him.

Nair watched as Cyrus leafed through the flurry of press releases that lay scattered across his mahogany desk. He approached, his footsteps soft but deliberate, and cleared his throat respectfully to catch the prime minister's attention.

"Sir," Nair began, his voice carrying a hint of his characteristic astuteness, "if I may be so bold, the issue of language is one that tugs fiercely at the heartstrings of our people. It's a mosaic of sentiment and identity, not just lines on a map."

Cyrus looked up, his expression revealing the fatigue and responsibility he carried. Nair continued, "A press statement is informative, yes, but the people need to see their leader. They need to feel your presence, hear your voice directly. You need to be the harbinger of this new chapter, not just the author behind the words."

There was a pause as the suggestion hung in the air. Nair could almost see the cogs turning in Cyrus's mind, evaluating, strategizing.

"Lead by example, they say," Nair added with a gentle yet mischievous smile, "and what better example than addressing your subjects in person? Your conviction will inspire theirs. A rally, perhaps, to share your vision and quell the tempest of anxieties this announcement has undoubtedly stirred."

Nair lingered for a moment, studying the reflective gaze of Cyrus, who seemed momentarily adrift in the sea of his thoughts. He took a breath before adding another layer to his counsel, one that he knew would either strike a chord or hit a nerve.

"Sir, if I may further advise," Nair said with a sense of careful reverence. "The heart of this linguistic turmoil beats loudest in Sindh. It is there that the soul of this decision will be either embraced or contested."

Cyrus's attention sharpened, the mention of Sindh drawing him back from the precipice of his contemplations. Nair stood firmly, emboldened by the importance of his proposition.

"Sindh," he continued, "is where the fervour runs deepest. It's where the people's sentiments are most inflamed, and understandably so. If you were to address a rally there, to stand amidst the very crowds that teeter between unrest and hope, it would send a powerful message."

He moved closer, ensuring the significance of his words was not missed. "It would show that you are not a leader who leads from the silence of high towers but one who walks amongst the turbulence of the streets. Your presence would signify a willingness to face the eye of the storm, to listen, and to lead from the front."

There was a truth in Nair's words that resonated within the walls of the office, a truth that Cyrus could not deny. Sindh was not just a city; it was the pulse of the nation's current unrest.

After a moment's consideration, a nod from Cyrus sealed the decision. "Make the arrangements, Mr. Nair. We shall go to Sindh," he said with a fresh resolve. "It's time the people see their leader standing with them, for them. It's time they heard our vision for unity from the heart of the struggle itself."

Nair nodded in acknowledgement, his eyes carrying the subtle pride of a confidant whose advice had been heeded. He turned to leave, already compiling the list of arrangements in his head. Sindh would not just be another rally; it would be a testament to Cyrus's leadership, a cornerstone in the legacy of a united nation.

Outside the confines of the prime minister's residence, the winds of change had begun to stir, carrying with them the murmurs of a restless nation. The reaction to Cyrus's unexpected decision was swift and varied.

The southern region, deeply proud and protective of its linguistic and cultural identity, was palpably discontented. Protests emerged in major cities like Madras and Hyderabad, where throngs of people gathered, chanting slogans, questioning the wisdom behind ignoring linguistic ties. Conversations in coffee houses were dominated by debates on the potential erosion of regional identities and the cultural richness of local languages. Leaders and scholars from the South, while acknowledging the broader vision, expressed concerns about the complexities and potential friction that could arise from merging historically distinct regions.

The state of Bombay, on the other hand, welcomed the announcement with open arms. Business tycoons, seeing the prospect of a more streamlined administrative structure, were optimistic about the opportunities it would present for trade and commerce. Intellectuals and progressive thinkers lauded Cyrus's vision of a united India beyond linguistic boundaries and believed that this decision would fuel the cosmopolitan ethos of the city even further.

The Northeast was a cauldron of mixed emotions. The diverse tapestry of tribes, each with its unique language and customs, faced a conundrum. Some felt that a geographically defined region would provide them with a larger platform to voice their concerns and be a part of the national narrative. Yet, others felt apprehensive, fearing that their unique cultural identities might get lost in the vast administrative expanse of the proposed Northeast region.

As newspapers flashed headlines, and radio stations broadcast heated discussions, India found itself at a significant crossroads. The country was in the throes of forming its identity, attempting to balance the rich tapestry of its regional cultures with the vision of a unified and progressive nation. The challenge now was in implementing this vision on the ground, ensuring that the mosaic of India remained as vibrant and diverse as ever, even as it moved forward as one.

Rajan penned an article and titled it, "Sindh: The Symphony of Languages." Sneha interviewed locals and found stories of resilience and hope amidst the turmoil.

Seventy-Two Hours after the Announcement

As the PM's aircraft descended, its engines wound down with a low whine, their echo hanging in the dry air of Sindh as Cyrus stepped onto the tarmac. The sun bore down relentlessly, its gaze unblinking and harsh, mirroring the scrutiny that Cyrus knew awaited him. The small airport was thronged by a sea of people, a mosaic of emotions painted on their faces—some with lines of tension, others with hopeful anticipation.

As his convoy snaked its way through the crowded streets, the cacophony of the city flooded in. The sharp staccato of slogans being chanted, the flurry of flags waving frenetically—some in protest, others in solidarity—created a tableau of the city's divided heart. Cyrus's eyes flitted across the faces in the crowd, absorbing the silent stories each one told.

The maidan was in sight now, an open field that today was a pulsating mass of humanity. People had gathered in droves, the atmosphere thick with anticipation. The stage was set against a backdrop of ancient trees, their branches swaying as if to whisper wisdom to those who would listen.

As Cyrus ascended the steps to the dais, the crowd swelled with a mix of cheers and boos, the discordant soundtrack of democracy in action.

He approached the microphone, his gaze steady, understanding the gravity of the moment.

"People of Sindh, citizens of our great nation, I stand before you today with a message that is crucial to the future of our beloved India. Over the past few weeks, I've been witness to passionate discussions and fervent pleas regarding the reformation of our state boundaries. A reformation based on linguistic differences. A division based on the languages we speak."

A murmur of agreement passed through the crowd. Cyrus continued, "I understand the depth of our cultural roots, the emotional bond we share with our mother tongues. But today, I ask you to think as an Indian first."

He paused, letting the import of his words sink in, then said, "Our nation, in its vastness, houses a plethora of languages, each beautiful, each sacred. But the strength of India does not lie in its divisions. It lies in its unity. It lies in its diverse but unified spirit."

A hush fell over the crowd, every eye fixed intently on Cyrus.

"If we begin to draw lines based on languages, where do we stop? Every dialect, every local tongue would demand its own space. And India, our glorious India, will be but a fragmented land of myriad broken pieces. It is not the legacy I wish to bequeath."

The intensity in Cyrus's voice was unmistakable. "History will judge our choices. If India is divided by languages, then the essence of our freedom struggle, the sacrifice of our forefathers, will be in vain."

He took a step forward, connecting deeply with his audience. "Imagine a future where a man in Bombay speaks Bengali without a shadow of prejudice. Envision a Karachi where Marathi echoes in the streets, not as a foreign tongue but as another melody in the symphony of our national identity."

He raised a hand to emphasize his point. "Our divisions will be geographical, to manage our vast lands more efficiently, not linguistic. The ethos of India is unity in diversity. It is this spirit that must guide our choices."

Cyrus concluded with a promise, "As your prime minister, it is my solemn vow to uphold the unity of India, to ensure that every voice is heard and every language celebrated. But as a nation, our unity will not be compromised."

A moment of silence followed. Then, from the back, a lone clap echoed, soon joined by another and another until the entire square reverberated with applause. It was clear: Cyrus's words had not just been heard, they had resonated.

The aftermath of the speech saw mixed reactions. While many praised Cyrus's vision for a unified India, there were factions that vehemently opposed his views. Debates raged in coffee houses, local gatherings, and newspapers. However, it was evident that Cyrus had struck a chord with the majority. His words became the talk of the nation, reaching even the remotest villages.

In the corridors of power, the reactions were equally divided. Ali Bhai and some of his associates were wary. "He's playing with fire," Ali Bhai said, pacing in his chamber. "Languages are deeply personal. People have fought for their linguistic rights. Cyrus may have overstepped this time."

Hamid, who had so far been observing quietly, remarked, "You underestimate him, Ali Bhai. He might have just prevented multiple insurgencies in the future."

Patel Sahib, in a discussion with other leaders of the Indian National Party, said, "This decision could go either way. But one thing is for sure—Cyrus has the courage to make tough decisions, and that's what this country needs right now."

Amidst all this, Gokhale's reaction was of particular interest. The man who usually championed the cause of the majority community had shown support for a unified, linguistic-diversity-friendly India. He was seen discussing the issue with some of his closest aides. "Cyrus might be on to something," he mused. "The idea is to keep

India undivided. Linguistic states might become a cause for further divisions, something we cannot afford."

Gokhale's support was a significant win for Cyrus. The two, having shared moments of camaraderie and conflict, were becoming unexpected allies in the journey of nation-building.

As days turned into weeks, it was clear that Cyrus's decision was becoming popular among the masses. Rallies supporting a geographically divided, linguistically unified India sprang up in various parts of the country. Songs praising the rich history of India's languages became anthems at these gatherings.

However, the journey was not without hurdles. Threats started pouring in from fringe elements. They felt betrayed and believed that their linguistic identity was being compromised. Cyrus's security was ramped up, but he refused to be intimidated.

Amidst all the tumult, Cyrus's leadership was steering India through one of its most challenging phases. His vision of harmony was slowly becoming the nation's shared dream. The path was treacherous, but the hope was alive.

The days that followed were marked by a series of events and gatherings, each designed to gauge the pulse of the nation and to bolster support for Cyrus's vision. He travelled extensively, addressing public meetings, interacting with scholars, and taking part in round table conferences. The aim was clear: to unify India's diverse populace under the banner of a shared identity while respecting and celebrating individual linguistic and cultural heritages.

In the southern city of Madras, he was met with a group of scholars and poets. They were keen to understand how Cyrus's vision of a geographically divided but linguistically unified nation would safeguard their rich Dravidian heritage.

One of the scholars, Dr. Ramanujam, posed a question, "Mr. Prime Minister, our literature and arts are deeply intertwined with our language. How do you see them flourish in your vision of India?"

Cyrus, ever the statesman, replied, "The beauty of India lies in its diversity. Just as the Ganga and the Yamuna meet and yet maintain their distinct identities, languages in India will coexist, influence one another, and flourish. No language will overshadow another. As prime minister, it is my duty to ensure that every linguistic group feels at home in any part of India."

In Punjab, he met with Sikhs who were concerned about the fate of their language and culture. To them, Cyrus promised protection of their religious sites and the promotion of Punjabi in schools and administration.

However, it was his visit to Bengal that was most crucial. Addressing a mammoth gathering in Calcutta, he said, "Bengal has been the intellectual heart of India. The literature, arts, and revolutionary spirit that have emanated from this land is unparalleled. I assure you, the Bengali language and culture will continue to thrive and flourish. An India without the essence of Bengal is unimaginable."

Back in Delhi, Gokhale was seen to be growing in prominence as a key ally to Cyrus, and many saw them as the twin pillars upon which the foundation of the new India was being built. Gokhale's RSD was instrumental in providing grassroots support to Cyrus's vision.

However, not everyone was in favour of this growing alliance. Ali Bhai, feeling increasingly sidelined, held clandestine meetings with his loyalists. Whispers of a potential challenge to Cyrus's leadership began to circulate.

One evening, as the sun painted the Delhi skyline with hues of orange and gold, Cyrus and Gokhale sat in the serene gardens of the prime minister's residence.

"Cyrus," began Gokhale, "I've heard troubling news. There are elements within the government who are unhappy with our association. They fear our combined influence."

Cyrus, sipping his chai, replied, "I am aware, Gokhaleji. But as long as our intentions are noble and for the good of the nation, we have nothing to fear."

Cyrus smiled weakly. "I only hope history proves me right."

Three Months after Declaration:

The first dual-language school opened in Karachi. Aisha and Priya, with their shared vision, were appointed its principals. Their endeavour, once a small community initiative, was now a beacon for the entire state.

Panditji and Gokhale, attending its inauguration, reflected, "It's never about the multitude of languages we speak but the singular language of unity and harmony we understand."

Gokhale, watching the children sing the national anthem in both languages, whispered to Panditji, "The melody of unity is the sweetest."

Panditji, his reservations still intact, couldn't help but admit, "Today, it indeed is."

Raja Krishnan, although having ceded some ground, felt content seeing his language flourish alongside others. A new era for Karachi was dawning.

As the chapter drew to a close, Karachi, once a hotspot of linguistic tension, was emerging as a model of coexistence. The path was fraught with challenges, but with dialogue, understanding, and compromise, unity was achievable. The journey of a nation navigating the treacherous waters of diversity continued unabated.

Chapter 7

DIPLOMACY IN SHADOWS

June 1950: The Prime Minister's Residence

The sprawling gardens of the prime minister's residence were a serene canvas of green, with the soft chittering of birds providing a gentle background melody. However, that tranquillity was abruptly disrupted as Nalini Sen rushed across the pathways, her saree billowing as her face portrayed a mix of anxiety and determination.

Cyrus, who was engrossed in a discussion with some cabinet members, noticed her hurried approach. He politely excused himself from the conversation and moved towards her, a look of concern etched on his face.

"Cyrus," she panted, slightly out of breath, "I've just been informed about an unscheduled, covert meeting between Hamid and the US ambassador. They met late last night at an undisclosed location in Delhi."

Cyrus raised an eyebrow, his calm demeanour giving way to alert seriousness. "Do we know the agenda?"

"We have snippets from our sources," Nalini replied. "It seems they discussed the ongoing geopolitics, especially concerning our relations with Israel. But there's more. They also touched upon trade sanctions and possible military pacts."

Cyrus sighed deeply, rubbing his temples. "This complicates matters. The US clearly sees an opportunity here."

Panditji, overhearing the exchange, chimed in, "It's a delicate game of chess we're playing, and the pieces are moving rapidly."

Cyrus nodded, looking out towards the garden's horizon, "We knew independence would come with its share of challenges, but the global theatre is evolving faster than we anticipated. We need to gather more intel and be ready for any ramifications."

Nalini nodded, determination renewed in her eyes. "I'll get our sources on it immediately and convene a meeting with the top brass in External Affairs. We need to ensure India's interests are protected at all costs."

As she hurried away to put things in motion, Cyrus reflected on the intricate web of international politics that now enmeshed India. The dream of a sovereign nation had become a reality but maintaining that sovereignty in the face of global superpowers was proving to be an ever-evolving challenge.

In the dimly lit corridors of the Indian Parliament, tension was palpable. The echoes of footsteps mingled with hushed voices. News of Hamid's secret rendezvous with the American ambassador had set the place on fire. The whispers grew louder, reaching the grand chamber where Cyrus sat contemplating the choices laid before him.

The room was already abuzz with the implications of the secret meeting when the radio's chimes, signalling an important announcement, caught everyone's attention. The newsreader's voice echoed in the otherwise silent room. "Breaking News: Rising tensions at the 38th parallel; indications of an imminent confrontation between North Korea and South Korea. Reports suggest that international powers might intervene."

The room went silent, all faces turned towards the radio, waiting for further updates. When none came, the volume of chatter gradually rose, each leader speculating and postulating about the possible ramifications.

In the midst of political intrigues in India, the world shifted its gaze to Asia's trembling frontier. A piercing cold wind ushered in June 1950, setting the stage for an explosive confrontation between North Korea and its southern neighbour.

The demarcation between North and South Korea was more than just a geographical boundary. It represented two opposing worldviews, two clashing ideologies: North Korea with its aggressive communist expansionism, and South Korea, nurturing seeds of democracy and free-market principles.

Without warning, North Korean troops, with their stark grey uniforms and red emblems, swept across the border, causing shock and panic. The verdant fields, once cultivated by generational farmers, now bore witness to a rapidly advancing invasion. South Korea's response was frantic and disarrayed. Their capital, Jindao, fell swiftly, echoing the harsh clamour of combat. Chatterjee approached Cyrus, her voice low and urgent. "Now we know what the meeting between Hamid and the US ambassador was about. They were seeking an understanding before the storm hit. Any guesses on India's role in this?"

Cyrus looked grim. "It's evident that the US wants our support, or at the very least, our neutrality in this upcoming conflict. Hamid's meeting with the ambassador was to gauge or possibly even negotiate our stance."

Panditji, who was deep in thought, mused aloud, "The situation on the Korean peninsula will shape the geopolitics of Asia."

Patel Sahib added, "Or they might be trying to use us as a mediator, considering our non-aligned approach and growing international reputation. They know our influence could either mitigate or exacerbate the situation."

Gokhale interjected, "Whatever the intent, we must tread carefully. The consequences of picking sides, especially in such a volatile region, could be severe."

Cyrus nodded. "We need more information, and quickly. I want insights into the meeting between Hamid and the ambassador. I also want to understand the international sentiment on this potential conflict and our possible roles in it."

The room buzzed with renewed energy.

In the ornate chambers of New Delhi, Cyrus's voice was composed, but the sharpness in his eyes was evident. "Get Hamid," he ordered his secretary firmly. "He owes us an explanation."

The secretary quickly left the room, and the air grew heavy with anticipation. The ornate clock on the wall seemed to tick louder, each second stretching, the stress of the impending confrontation making everyone tense.

Minutes passed. The large wooden double doors finally opened, revealing a flustered Hamid, escorted by the secretary. As Hamid entered, his eyes darted around the room, taking in the evident tension.

"Hamid," began Cyrus in a tone that suggested restrained frustration, "we are in the dark about your secret meeting with the US ambassador. What were you discussing that you felt the need to keep us out of the loop?"

Hamid cleared his throat, attempting to maintain his composure. "Sir, it was a general diplomatic meeting, nothing specific."

Patel Sahib intervened, his voice authoritative. "Do not play games with us. The timing of your 'general' meeting, just before the news of an imminent conflict in Korea, seems more than coincidental. What did the ambassador say? What were the terms discussed?"

Hamid hesitated for a moment, then sighed, his shoulders slumping. "The US is interested in our stance, should a conflict arise in Korea. They wanted to know if we'd be open to supporting them or if we'd remain neutral."

Chatterjee scoffed, "And you thought this wasn't vital enough to share with us immediately?"

Gokhale added, "It's clear they want something from us. It's also clear we're in a position of leverage. We must use this to our advantage."

Hamid's voice was tinged with a mix of frustration and desperation. "We're at a juncture where India must choose its friends carefully. The Americans are offering aid, a significant credit line. In return, they want us to allow them to set up a military base near Vishakapatnam."

Cyrus, his face reddening, countered, "This isn't just about money, Hamid. This is about our sovereignty. You want to bring foreign troops to our land? For what? So we can be embroiled in their wars?"

Hamid slammed his hand on the mahogany table. "This is about survival, Cyrus! About aligning ourselves with powers that can help us grow. You've seen the reports. South Korea is on the brink of collapse. The Americans can halt the North Koreans."

Staring intently at Hamid, Cyrus whispered menacingly, "You forget your place, Finance Minister. Your domain is the economy, not foreign policy."

Hamid, breathing heavily, replied, "Our economy is intertwined with our foreign policy. If India doesn't make the right alliances now, our future will be dictated by those who do."

The room was thick with unease. The burden of the decisions, the lives affected, and the fate of nations hung in the balance.

Outside, rain began to pour, casting a gloomy backdrop to their intense debate.

Suddenly, Panditji intervened, sensing the simmering tension. "Gentlemen, the Korean conflict affects us all. But we must remember that unity is our strength."

Cyrus turned to him. "Panditji, Hamid here believes that our salvation lies in allying ourselves with the Americans, in drawing them onto our soil. Can we afford such a gamble?"

Panditji sighed. "The world is changing, Cyrus. The embers of World War II have ignited the Cold War. We must tread carefully, choosing our path with prudence."

Hamid interjected, "We can't remain neutral forever, Panditji. The Americans can be our allies, providing us with the resources we desperately need."

Cyrus, exasperated, shot back, "And what happens when they leave, Hamid? Once Vishakapatnam becomes a target for our enemies? Have you considered the repercussions?"

The debate raged on, echoing the conflicts tearing the world apart.

Hamid stood by the window, trying to put on a façade of calm. He looked out at the manicured gardens, taking a deep breath before turning to face Cyrus.

Cyrus's gaze was unwavering, his stern demeanour emphasized by the dim lighting. "Hamid," he began, "I have always considered you a confidant and a vital member of this government. But your recent actions... they are not just against protocol, they are against the very fabric of our unity and sovereignty."

Hamid took a defensive stance. "Cyrus, I only did what I believed was right for the nation."

Vikram, who had been silent till now, interrupted, "By meeting the US ambassador secretly? By not consulting the cabinet?"

Chatterjee added with a pointed look, "Such actions are dangerous, Hamid. They can easily be misinterpreted."

Gokhale interjected, "They could be seen as treasonous."

Hamid shot her a sharp look, but before he could retort, Cyrus continued, "Hamid, I respect your passion and dedication to our country. But such unilateral decisions can't be tolerated. This is a democracy, and we are here to work together, not in silos."

Hamid's face showed a mix of anger and frustration. "So, what now?" he asked bitterly.

Cyrus leaned forward, his voice a low, controlled growl. "This is your last warning, Hamid. I won't tolerate any more breaches of trust. Remember, the nation always comes first."

Hamid nodded curtly. "Understood."

The room remained silent for a few moments, the seriousness of the confrontation still hanging heavy. The path forward for India was challenging, and trust amongst its leaders was paramount.

As the night grew darker, the room seemed to shrink, enveloped in the heavy cloak of tension. The silences between the exchanges were as telling as the words themselves. But there was more to the story than just the power play in that room.

The next day, as dawn broke, news arrived that American and North Korean forces had engaged in a fierce battle just eighty kilometres from Busan. The entire region was on a knife's edge.

The urgency of the situation was palpable. Cyrus, Nalini, Hamid, Panditji, and Vikram convened once more.

"North Korea is gaining ground," Hamid began. "Our delay could prove costly."

With a deep breath, Cyrus began, "After considerable thought and consultation with the relevant ministries, I've decided that India will extend only humanitarian aid to South Korea. We will not, under any circumstances, get involved militarily."

There was a split-second silence before the room erupted in reactions.

Patel Sahib, always a man of action, responded first. "Cyrus, it's a delicate situation. Are we prepared for the backlash?"

Panditji sighed. "In an already fragile global political scenario, this might send mixed signals to our allies and adversaries alike."

Vikram interjected, "It's a strategic move. I stand by it. Our armed forces need to be focused on our borders and internal security. South Korea's battle is not ours to fight."

Nalini, added, "It's not about not supporting South Korea. It's about focusing on our immediate needs. We're still a young nation, grappling with our internal issues. This decision is about preservation."

Chatterjee, thinking of the international press and public opinion, said, "We need to handle the messaging very carefully. The world must know that our decision stems from a place of neutrality and peace, not indifference."

Hamid, surprisingly, nodded in agreement. "As much as I've disagreed with some decisions, Cyrus, this one makes sense. We can't spread ourselves thin. Not now."

Cyrus surveyed the room, absorbing the feedback. "I understand the implications and the potential repercussions. But right now, our nation's stability and growth are paramount. We must prioritize."

Everyone nodded, realizing the enormity of their collective decision. They were shaping the foreign policy of a nascent nation, making decisions that would echo through history.

Late into the afternoon, a resolution was reached. India would send humanitarian aid to South Korea and would voice its concerns on global platforms. However, the proposal to allow a US military base in Vishakapatnam was shelved — for now.

Nair was intently reading through a stack of documents when a firm voice interrupted his concentration. He looked up to see Cyrus, eyes resolute, walking briskly towards him.

"Cyrus, how can I assist you?" Nair asked, adjusting his glasses and placing the papers down.

"I need you to set up a direct line with Premier Lee of South Korea. Immediately," Cyrus commanded, the urgency in his voice unmistakable.

Nair was taken aback. It wasn't every day that the prime minister made such a direct request, especially one involving international communication. The room buzzed with whispers as everyone took note of the unfolding scene.

"Any specific topic, sir?" Nair probed cautiously, already motioning for his staff to get the call ready.

Cyrus paused, taking a deep breath. "The current crisis, Nair. It's time we clarified our stance."

Nair nodded, understanding the severity of the situation. "Understood. I'll have it arranged right away."

As Nair's assistants scrambled to make the necessary arrangements, the room grew tense in anticipation. They all recognized that the ensuing conversation would have significant consequences, not just for India, but potentially, for the entire geopolitical landscape.

The large wooden doors to the prime minister's office slowly closed, and a hushed silence enveloped the room. Everyone's gaze was fixed on Cyrus.

Chatterjee was the first to break the silence. "Sir, the hotline to South Korea is ready."

Cyrus nodded, steeling himself. "Connect me."

The room watched intently as the dial tone buzzed, waiting for the premier of South Korea to answer. Within moments, the line clicked, and a voice came through. "This is Premier Lee."

"Cyrus Engineer here," the Indian prime minister responded, his voice firm but compassionate.

"I wanted to personally inform you that while we cannot involve ourselves militarily, India will fully support South Korea with humanitarian aid. We stand by our friends in their hour of need."

Premier Lee paused for a moment, evidently touched by the gesture. "Prime Minister Engineer, I can't express my gratitude enough. This means a lot to us. During these trying times, your support not only strengthens our resolve but reminds us that we aren't alone."

Cyrus replied, "It's a new dawn for our nations, Premier Lee. In these testing times, our unity and friendship will shine the brightest. Remember, the spirit of humanity binds us all."

The call ended, and the room echoed with the finality of the decision made. Everyone knew that the repercussions of this choice would reverberate on the global stage. But for now, they had the satisfaction of knowing that they had stood by a friend.

And as the night drew on, in that room filled with leaders and decision-makers, there was a quiet acknowledgement that history was in the making.

When the decision was announced, reactions poured in from across the globe. While some lauded India's balanced approach, others felt it was a missed opportunity.

As the meeting drew to a close, Cyrus stared out of the window, watching the sun set over the horizon. The orange hues seemed to cast long, reflective shadows in the room, and perhaps, on the decisions made therein.

Panditji approached him, placing a reassuring hand on his shoulder. "You know, my friend, every leader has their crucible moment. This might be yours."

Cyrus smiled faintly. "I never imagined leading our nation would involve making choices on such a grand scale. It's daunting."

Patel Sahib chimed in, "But remember, every choice we make now is setting a precedent. We're not just guiding our nation for today but setting the course for generations to come."

Chatterjee added, "Both domestically and internationally, the world is watching us closely. The steps we take, the decisions we make, they're not just for now. They are chapters in the history we are writing."

Cyrus nodded, taking in their words. He could feel the burden of responsibility pressing on him. "This nation was born out of hope and a dream for a brighter future. I intend to honour that dream."

As everyone left the room, the stillness was profound. In the corridors of power, decisions had been made, and as day turned into night, the young prime minister of a newly independent nation stood resolute, aware that his leadership would be etched into the annals of history.

Chapter 8

THE VEIL OF TREACHERY

October 9, 1950:
The Prime Minister's Office

Cyrus sat behind the grand desk in his office, reading reports and making notations for his cabinet meeting later that day, when there was a sharp rap on his door.

"Come in," he called, without looking up.

The door opened to reveal an uneasy-looking General Mehta, the head of India's intelligence agency. He seldom looked perturbed, but today was different. In his hand, he held a sealed envelope with a red wax stamp, symbolizing the utmost confidentiality.

Cyrus immediately picked up on the tension. "General, what brings you here at this hour?"

General Mehta cleared his throat, "We've received… unsettling news from Moscow, Mr. Prime Minister."

Cyrus raised an eyebrow. "Go on."

"We have an Indian businessman," Mehta hesitated, "captured in Russia. They've labelled him a spy."

Cyrus felt a chill run down his spine. "Who is it?"

General Mehta slid the envelope across the desk. "Details are within. But it's imperative you know, his capture wasn't part of any sanctioned operation to the best of my knowledge. If the Russians believe otherwise…"

"It could be the end of our diplomatic ties." Cyrus finished the sentence, the intensity of the circumstances not lost on him.

He broke the seal and read the brief. His face turned several shades paler. "This… this is disastrous."

General Mehta nodded gravely. "Moscow expects an official response from us by tomorrow. They've hinted at… implications if we don't handle this delicately."

Cyrus looked up, meeting Mehta's gaze. "We need to arrange an emergency meeting. This could escalate beyond our control."

"As you wish, Mr. Prime Minister," Mehta responded.

"And General," Cyrus added as Mehta turned to leave, "let's keep this under wraps. The last thing we need is panic and speculations."

The general nodded, and with a swift salute, left the room.

Cyrus leaned back in his chair, letting out a deep sigh. The fate of the nation's diplomatic ties with a superpower, and the life of a captured agent, now hung precariously in the balance. He hoped he was up to the challenge that lay ahead.

Cyrus picked up the secure phone line on his desk, pressing the direct button to connect to the External Affairs Minister, Nalini Sen.

"Nalini," he said without preamble, "we have a situation. I need you in my office, now. Also, please inform Dr. Rao and Mr. Joshi to be present as well."

The line was silent for a split second before she responded. "I'm on my way."

Within minutes, the door to his office opened again, revealing a slightly out-of-breath Nalini. Behind her, entered the defence minister, Vikram Joshi, and the national security advisor, Dr. Rao.

"What's happened?" Nalini inquired, her eyes darting to the open envelope on the desk.

Cyrus pushed the brief towards her. As she read, her normally composed features contorted with shock. Joshi and Dr. Rao exchanged worried glances, awaiting their turn to be briefed.

"We can't let this escalate," Nalini finally said, looking up.

Joshi snorted, "The Russians have our man, and they label him a spy! How do you propose we not let this escalate?!"

Dr. Rao intervened, "Let's not jump to conclusions. We need a plan."

Cyrus nodded. "First, we need to ascertain why our operative was in Russia if it wasn't a sanctioned operation. What was he doing there?"

Nalini flipped through the pages. "It seems he was tracing some personal family connections, something related to a past inheritance."

"That's a thin excuse to be in Moscow, especially given his background," Joshi mused.

Cyrus pondered for a moment. "We need a two-fold approach. Firstly, we must understand the circumstances that led to his capture. Secondly, we need to diplomatically handle the Russians. We cannot afford an international incident."

Nalini chimed in, "We need to send an envoy. Someone they respect but not someone too high-ranking to be seen as a desperate move."

Dr. Rao suggested, "What about Ambassador Meher? He has good relations with the Russian administration."

Cyrus nodded in agreement. "Arrange for Meher to be on the next flight to Moscow. In the meantime, I want a full briefing on this so-called operative.

Everything, from his childhood to what he had for breakfast yesterday."

The room filled with affirmative murmurs. Everyone's faces reflected the intensity of the predicament.

As the group moved towards the door, Joshi paused. "Cyrus, you realize if we handle this wrong, it's not just our ties with Russia that are at stake. The world is watching. One wrong move and our newly gained independence will be overshadowed by an international fiasco."

Cyrus looked squarely at Vikram. "I'm well aware, Vikram. But we have faced challenges before. We will face this one head-on as well."

With that proclamation, the team got into action, hoping to avert a crisis that threatened to cast a shadow on India's fledgling sovereignty.

The evening was darkening as the chaos inside the prime minister's house deepened. Whispers of the captured spy echoed through the hallways. Reporters had already gathered outside, seeking any drop of information they could glean.

Inside the war room, a dedicated space for emergency meetings, the core team assembled. Maps of Moscow, intelligence reports, and telecommunication set-ups crowded the area.

Cyrus sat at the head of the long mahogany table. His gaze unfaltering, he said, "Let's ensure there's no leak from our end. We need to control the narrative."

Nalini, already coordinating with the media team, added, "Our statement should focus on the personal nature of our operative's trip, emphasizing that it had nothing to do with official government business."

Dr. Rao interjected, "But we must be cautious. Even a hint of doubt could turn international sentiment against us."

Amidst the discussion, a junior officer entered hesitantly. "Sir, Ambassador Meher is on a secure line from Moscow."

The room fell silent as Cyrus picked up the receiver. The next few minutes seemed like hours. His face was inscrutable as he listened, only nodding occasionally.

He finally placed the receiver down. "Ambassador Meher has been granted an audience with the Russian foreign minister tomorrow morning. But we must be prepared for a long negotiation. The Russians are seeing this as a breach of trust."

Joshi clenched his fists. "We cannot let them dictate terms. Our sovereignty is at stake."

Cyrus took a deep breath. "We won't. But neither can we approach this as an act of aggression. We need to tread a thin line."

As minutes turned into hours, backchannel communications between New Delhi and Moscow intensified. Sleep-deprived officials worked round the clock, fuelled by the urgency of the situation.

October 11, 1950: Kremlin, Moscow

Ambassador Meher stepped out of his chauffeured car, taking a deep breath as he looked up at the majestic walls of the Kremlin. It was a chilly October morning in Moscow. The sky was a pale grey, and the air was filled with the faint scent of burning wood. The golden domes of the churches within the Kremlin complex glistened against the dull backdrop, with the imposing red brick walls standing as silent witnesses to countless secrets and events that had shaped the course of Russian history.

Guarded by the iconic Spasskaya Tower, the entrance seemed even more foreboding today. The rhythmic sound of marching soldiers added to the imposing atmosphere as they performed their routine guard change.

Meher's heart raced a little faster. The matter at hand was delicate, and the Russians had every reason to be displeased. The spy issue had brought Indo-Russian relations to a precipice, and it was his responsibility to ensure that the balance did not tip towards a breakdown.

As he walked through the vast corridors, the echoes of his footsteps were a constant reminder of the magnitude of the situation. He was ushered into a lavishly decorated room where the Russian foreign minister, Ivanov, awaited him.

Foreign Minister Ivanov did not stand as Meher entered. His cold, piercing eyes remained fixed on a file before him. "Ambassador Meher," he began in a frosty tone, "Your country's actions are seen as nothing short of a betrayal. We had expectations from India, and this... incident with the spy undermines our trust."

Meher cleared his throat, choosing his words carefully. "Minister Ivanov, we are here to clear any misunderstandings and ensure that our long-standing friendship remains intact."

Ivanov leaned back, folding his hands. "This is not just about understanding, Ambassador. This is about trust. And actions have consequences. The president will decide the fate of the spy."

The heavy silence that followed was finally broken by distant chimes from the Spasskaya Tower. As Meher left the Kremlin, he realized that the road ahead was treacherous, and the stakes for India had never been higher.

October 12, 1950: New Delhi

Meanwhile, news of the captured operative spread like wildfire. International dailies splashed headlines, some siding with India's claim of innocence with others hinting at a darker espionage tale.

But amidst the political storm, a human story was emerging. Reports began to focus on the captured man's family, his childhood, and his alleged quest to find his Russian lineage.

That night, as a particularly intense discussion was winding down, Nalini approached Cyrus. "You know, amidst all this chaos, we're forgetting one thing."

Cyrus looked up, eyebrows raised in inquiry.

"The man. The so-called businessman. Behind the titles and accusations, there's a human being who is scared, alone, and trapped in a foreign land."

Cyrus sighed, rubbing his temples. "You're right, Nalini. But our primary concern has to be the greater good. If that means making difficult decisions…"

Mr. Nair scratched his head and mused, "Spies, spies everywhere, and not a single one to fetch me a decent bottle of vodka from Moscow."

Cyrus laughed. "Trust you to think of alcohol in the midst of a crisis…" He trailed off.

In the middle of the next day, a coded message was delivered to Cyrus. Deciphering it, he found that it came from his counterpart in Moscow. The content was brief but earth-shattering: "Hamid was behind this. He told us to execute the spy."

Cyrus's mind raced. Hamid? His trusted ally, a member of his own cabinet? Was this some sort of political gambit, or was Hamid acting on his own accord, possibly fuelled by personal motives? Or, perhaps even more unsettling, was this information an attempt by the Russians to further destabilize India's fledgling government?

Gathering his core team again in the war room, Cyrus relayed the news. The room, always a place of tension, grew ice-cold.

Joshi was the first to break the silence. "This is a direct betrayal! If this is true, then Hamid has not only betrayed us but the whole nation!"

Nalini interjected, "Let's not jump to conclusions. It could be misinformation to divert our attention. The Russians are masters at this game."

Dr. Rao, deep in thought, looked up. "But what if it's true? This could change everything. The ramifications are enormous, not just for us but for every political move India makes henceforth."

The discussions were endless. Was Hamid acting alone or representing a faction within the government? Was this a bid to oust Cyrus and change the course of India's future?

The room was thick with tension as past and present decisions collided, setting the stage for the future course of the young nation.

Cyrus leaned forward, his voice low but firm, "Nalini, Joshi, Dr. Rao, the information about Hamid's dealings is extremely sensitive. It could have significant implications not just for our government but for the nation's standing in the global arena."

Nalini nodded in agreement. "Absolutely, Cyrus. Such information, if leaked prematurely, could cause unnecessary panic and speculation. It's imperative that we keep this under wraps until we have irrefutable evidence."

Joshi added, "Secrecy is paramount. We need to handle this with utmost discretion to avoid any potential backlash or misunderstanding."

Cyrus's eyes swept over his trusted ministers. "We must investigate this thoroughly and discreetly. We cannot afford to act on mere suspicions. The credibility of our government and the stability of our political landscape depend on how we manage this situation."

Nalini interjected, "I'll ensure that our intelligence networks are on high alert and that any further information is funnelled directly to us. We need to stay ahead of this."

Joshi nodded in agreement. "And I'll see to it that our defence channels are prepared for any unforeseen consequences. We'll keep our strategies close until we have a clear course of action."

Cyrus, reassured by their responses, concluded the meeting with a sense of resolute urgency. "Keep me updated on any developments. We must act swiftly and strategically to navigate this crisis."

October 14, 1950: The PM's Office

Dr. Rao handed Cyrus a file the next day. It contained communications, intercepted by Indian intelligence, between Hamid and certain high-ranking American officials. The contents were explicit: Hamid had been promised support, both political and financial, should he take a stance that favoured American interests in the region. Cyrus immediately summoned a meeting of the cabinet along with Patel Sahib and Panditji, specifically leaving out Ali Bhai.

As Cyrus went through the documents, it became clear that Hamid had his eyes set on being in the good books of the Americans. He saw the USA, with its immense military and economic prowess, as the real power player in the post-World War II world. Russia, with its socialist ideologies, was a direct threat to the capitalist interests that Hamid subtly championed.

A note in the file mentioned a secret meeting in Karachi, where Hamid supposedly met with a CIA operative. The agenda? To ensure that India, while officially non-aligned, would subtly tilt towards the West in its policies.

Cyrus felt a sinking feeling in his stomach at this deception. "So, he wanted to avoid negotiations with Russia, not out of patriotism but to realign India's geopolitical stance," he whispered to himself. "Summon Hamid immediately," he yelled.

He decided to have another confrontation with Hamid. This time with evidence in hand.

"You traded the safety of our nation for personal gain!" accused Cyrus, his voice echoing in the chamber.

Hamid, trying to retain his composure, replied, "It's not about personal gain, Cyrus. It's about aligning ourselves with the future. America is the future. We need their support if we are to emerge as a global powerhouse."

"You sacrificed a life, Hamid! A life!" thundered Cyrus.

"We always have to make sacrifices for the greater good," Hamid responded coldly.

The room was charged with tension. Both leaders, with their own visions for India, stood at odds. The fate of their relationship, and perhaps the direction of the nation, hung in the balance.

In the grand chamber, surrounded by portraits of maharajas, Cyrus faced Hamid. "You have overstepped your boundaries, Hamid. Conducting covert discussions with foreign powers? And even compromising an Indian life?"

Hamid, though defiant, lacked his usual arrogance. "I did what I believed was right for the country, and for our place in the world," he retorted.

Nalini Sen adjusted her glasses and interrupted, "While the manner of communication could've been better, Hamid, the implications of what you've done are far-reaching. The US's ambitions in Asia are clear, and you've played right into their hands!"

Mrs. Chatterjee voiced the concern in everyone's minds. "The bigger question is—what else don't we know about? What other arrangements are in place?"

Hamid's gaze darted around the room, sensing the growing animosity. "Listen," he began, trying to remain calm, "we all have India's best interests at heart. The conversations with the US were exploratory at best. But you must understand the pressure at the time of independence. Choices were made."

Cyrus spoke up, his voice firm. Transparency and trust are paramount. This isn't the time for personal ambitions."

Hamid, his patience frayed, launched into a barely veiled taunt. "Cyrus, while you sit here contemplating the finer points of governance, I'm out there making real decisions," he said, his voice laced with a mix of derision and exasperation. "I don't have the luxury of learning on the job as you do."

Cyrus, taken aback by Hamid's audacity, struggled to maintain his composure. The atmosphere in the room grew tense, with every cabinet member keenly aware of the escalating confrontation.

"You may play at being prime minister," Hamid continued, his words sharp as knives, "but some of us have actual work to do. Securing investments, building trade relationships, ensuring our nation's economy doesn't stagnate while you learn the ropes."

The brazen challenge to Cyrus's authority was unprecedented. His colleagues, including stalwarts like Patel Sahib and Gokhale, exchanged glances of disbelief and discomfort.

But Hamid, unfazed and perhaps emboldened by Cyrus's response, leaned forward, his gaze unyielding. "A united front led by inexperience and hesitation is no front at all, Cyrus. You may sit at the head of this table, but don't mistake your position for absolute authority."

The room fell silent, the tension thick enough to slice. This was no longer a mere policy disagreement; it was an open revolt against Cyrus's leadership, a moment that threatened to upend the delicate balance of power within the government.

With a calmness that belied the turmoil within, Cyrus finally spoke. "Mr. Hamid," he began, his voice resonating with a quiet but unmistakable authority, "your services to this nation are no longer required. You are dismissed from your position as finance minister, effective immediately."

Cyrus gave a subtle nod to the guards stationed discreetly at the door. They stepped forward, their presence a silent but clear indication that the decision was non-negotiable. As they approached Hamid, the reality of the situation set in—he was being escorted out, his tenure as finance minister abruptly ended.

Hamid's face had turned ashen, but defiance sparkled in his eyes. "Panditji," he retorted, "you seem to forget the arrangements that were made. This wasn't our deal. Ali Bhai won't take this lightly, and you know it. It was on these terms that we worked to keep India united!"

Cyrus's gaze turned to Panditji, seeking answers. "Arrangement?"

Patel Sahib cut in, "Arrangement or no arrangement, there's a chain of command. One can't simply go rogue!"

The room echoed with Cyrus's declaration. Hamid, his dreams crushed, was escorted out.

The turmoil of the past few hours had taken a toll on Cyrus, but he knew he had one final play to make. He needed to speak directly to the Russian president. Using his diplomatic channels, an urgent call was set up. As the phone rang, Cyrus took a deep breath.

"Mr. President," Cyrus began, his voice firm but respectful. "India is at a crossroads. Our land has been a witness to great empires and age-old civilizations. Yet, the echoes of the Korean War reverberate even in our corridors. Your dispute with the US over North Korea is drawing lines across the globe."

The Russian president, his voice cold as Siberian ice, responded, "Mr. Prime Minister, every nation has to pick a side. Neutrality is but a fleeting illusion."

Cyrus felt the challenge in those words but stood his ground. "We've just gained our independence,

Mr. President. We have no intention of becoming a pawn in a larger game. Your conflict with the Americans, your race for nuclear dominance, it's not our fight. But our businessman, detained on your soil, he is our concern."

The president took a moment. Then he said, "That businessman, as you call him, was found with documents that aren't... shall we say, tourist guides. What assurance can you offer that India will not tilt towards the Americans?"

Cyrus, drawing from his deepest reservoirs of diplomacy, said, "Our only tilt is towards our people. Our history reflects our belief in sovereignty and non-alignment. While the US and USSR engage in proxy wars, like in Korea, India seeks peace. We don't want American bases, nor do we want to be swayed by their capitalist charms. But we also won't be pressured into decisions by threats or detainments."

A tense silence lingered.

The Russian president finally broke the silence. "You're a brave man, Mr. Prime Minister. I'll give you that. All right, we'll release your businessman. But remember, in this rapidly changing world, alliances can shift like desert sands."

Cyrus, sensing the closure he so desperately needed, replied, "Thank you, Mr. President. India remembers its friends and its commitments. Peace be with you."

As the line went dead, Cyrus leaned back, the tension momentarily lifted. The path ahead was uncertain, but for now, a crisis had been averted.

The subdued light in the room seemed a little brighter, as if acknowledging the small victory Cyrus had achieved in his conversation with the Russian president. Outside, a tempest was brewing, both literally and metaphorically. The rain started as a gentle drizzle but soon turned torrential, echoing the tumultuous political landscape of 1950.

Cyrus's close aide, Vishwanathan, entered the room with a file in his hand. "Sir, the reports from the Intelligence Bureau regarding Hamid's dealings with the Americans are here."

Cyrus opened the file, his fingers trembling slightly. The contents confirmed his worst fears. Hamid was playing a dangerous game, trying to leverage India's strategic position for personal gains and aligning with the Americans against the Russians.

A knot formed in Cyrus's stomach. The challenge was not only external but internal. The very fabric of the young nation was at risk, threatened by its own leaders.

Vishwanathan looked at Cyrus, his eyes filled with concern. "Sir, this could be catastrophic. If this information leaks to the public, it will cause chaos."

Cyrus nodded. "I'm well aware, Vishwanathan. But we must remember, the essence of democracy is transparency. We can't hide this, but we must deal with it carefully."

As the two talked, there was a knock on the door, and Panditji entered, his face grim. "Cyrus, we have another situation. The Americans have sent an envoy. They want to discuss a 'potential partnership' with us."

Cyrus sighed, the burden of leadership pressing down on him once again. The US, sensing a shift after the revelation of Hamid's dealings and Cyrus's conversation with the Russian president, was making its move.

Panditji continued, "They've come bearing gifts—promises of aid, infrastructure development, and military support. But at what cost?"

Cyrus looked out of the window, the rain pouring outside reflecting the storm inside his mind. "We tread on a razor's edge, Panditji. Our non-alignment policy is more than just a stance; it's our identity. If we lean too much on one side, we might lose our balance and fall."

Panditji nodded. "And yet, we can't ignore the global realities. The world is polarizing, and we must navigate our path without losing our essence."

Cyrus closed the file in front of him, his decision made. "Arrange a meeting with the American envoy tomorrow. Let's hear them out. But remember, we will not be swayed by promises or threats. India will chart its own course."

As the leaders prepared for the challenges of the next day, the city outside tried to recover from the onslaught of rain. Both the nation and its capital were learning to weather storms, holding on to hope and resilience.

The next day, the grand ballroom of the prime minister's residence was bathed in golden hues as the evening sun streamed through its ornate windows.

Cyrus was seated at the head of a long teak table, sipping on his Darjeeling tea, when the American envoy, Richard Donnelly, entered. Tall, broad-shouldered, with sharp features and slicked-back silver hair, Donnelly was an imposing presence.

Without much ado, Donnelly began, "Mr. Prime Minister, the world is at a crucial juncture. There are powers seeking to rewrite the global order, and we believe India has a critical role to play. The US wants India by its side. We urge you to join the NATO alliance. It's an offer of friendship, an unbreakable pact that will ensure the safety and prosperity of your nation."

Cyrus carefully considered his words. "Mr. Donnelly, I understand the significance of the offer. But I must remind you, I am but a temporary guardian of this young nation. My tenure is short-lived, and such monumental decisions should be the prerogative of a full-term government chosen by the people."

Donnelly leaned forward, his blue eyes intense. "With all due respect, Mr. Prime Minister, the world won't wait. The Russians, they're not to be trusted. Their intentions are never clear. This is your chance to align with the right side of history."

Cyrus took a deep breath. "Our history has taught us to be non-aligned and to judge actions, not intentions. While I appreciate the hand of friendship you extend, our current stance of non-alignment serves our interests best. After our general elections, it will be up to the Parliament to decide our path."

Donnelly looked disappointed, but his demeanour remained respectful. "Very well, Mr. Prime Minister. We respect your decision. But remember, the offer stands. The United States believes in a strong and prosperous India."

Twenty-Four Hours Later: Meeting Room, Prime Minister's Office

The meeting room was filled with the murmurs of ministers and advisors discussing the latest political happenings.

The room's thick curtains blocked any hint of the sun, and the air inside felt tense. The long oval table was surrounded by leaders, officials, and diplomats, all of them engrossed in the ongoing discussion when Nalini, with an air of grace and authority, stepped forward.

She cleared her throat, making everyone look up in anticipation. "Cyrus," she began with a voice that commanded attention despite its softness, "we have just received a rather disconcerting piece of evidence from our Russian counterparts." She paused, gauging the room's reaction. "They have furnished proof, unequivocal in nature, that links the spy with none other than the British high commissioner, Field Marshal Claud Bernard."

Whispers filled the room. Faces reflected surprise, confusion, and for some, validation of long-held suspicions.

Field Marshal Claud Bernard was no ordinary envoy. Appointed as the first British ambassador to independent India by Prime Minister Atlee, his reputation preceded him. Tall and imposing, Bernard was in his late fifties, with sharp, hawkish features that rarely gave away his emotions. His silver hair was always impeccably styled, his moustache trimmed to perfection. His piercing blue eyes seemed to miss nothing, and he carried himself with the air of someone who was used to command and respect. He was known for his strategic brilliance in World War II and his diplomatic finesse during the post-war period. Many viewed his appointment as a clear signal from Britain—a gesture that indicated their keenness to establish strong, renewed ties with an independent India.

Cyrus, absorbing the revelation, asked, "Nalini, how reliable is this information?"

Nalini nodded. "It comes directly from the Russian ambassador, with substantial evidence that our intelligence has verified independently."

Cyrus's gaze hardened. "Then it's imperative we confront the field marshal. Nalini, summon him to my office immediately. If these allegations hold any truth, it could redefine our relationship with the UK."

Nalini acknowledged with a nod, and as she left to relay the message, the room was once again abuzz with speculations and concerns about the diplomatic storm that loomed ahead.

Everyone turned to look when Field Marshal Bernard, dressed in his distinct British attire, walked in. The ambassador stood tall, his eyes scanning the room as he walked in with the composed manner of someone used to command. A stunned silence followed, replacing the previous buzz.

Bernard offered a curt nod in acknowledgement. "Prime Minister," he greeted.

Cyrus, without returning the pleasantries, gestured towards the chair opposite him. "Field Marshal Bernard, please sit."

Bernard hesitated for a second before seating himself, his military poise evident. "To what do I owe the pleasure of this… unexpected meeting, Prime Minister?"

"Marshal," Cyrus began, leaning forward with both hands clasped on the table, "we have received some distressing information linking you to the spy apprehended by the Russians recently. The evidence suggests a deeper involvement of the British government."

Bernard's eyes narrowed, betraying a hint of irritation. "Prime Minister, I assure you I'm not aware of any such links. Perhaps this is some sort of misunderstanding or an unfortunate coincidence?"

Cyrus, unyielding, continued, "The Russian ambassador has furnished undeniable proof of your connection to the spy. Now, I'll be straightforward. I need answers. Not stories. Not deflections."

For a moment, Bernard was silent, measuring Cyrus's determination. He then exhaled slowly, choosing his words. "Mr. Prime Minister, Britain has had a long relationship with India. While our countries have had differences in the past, it's a new era. I cannot imagine why Britain would jeopardize our relations by indulging in such an act."

Cyrus leaned in, his voice unwavering. "That's not an answer, Bernard. What I need from you now is transparency. If there's been a transgression, admit it. We can find a way to manage the fallout. But if you choose to continue this dance of evasion, I assure you, it won't bode well for our diplomatic ties."

Bernard looked into Cyrus's eyes, a mixture of wariness and contemplation evident. "Prime Minister, there's more to this story than just the events of recent days. I believe, to understand the current predicament, we must journey back to a pivotal moment before independence."

Cyrus leaned back in his chair, intrigued. "Go on."

"In the spring of 1945, as World War II was nearing its end, there was a private meeting at 10 Downing Street, one that was meant to remain a secret for decades," Bernard began. "I was there, along with Prime Minister Atlee and Lord Williamson."

May 1, 1945: 10 Downing Street, London

A lavish room, adorned with plush red carpets and walls lined with age-old portraits, hosted a trio of men discussing the future of India. A large oak table stood in the centre, upon which rested a map of India, partition lines being drawn and redrawn.

Atlee leaned forward, his fingers interlaced, eyes piercing through his thick glasses. "William," he began, addressing Williamson, "you are entrusted with our exit from India. This isn't just about withdrawal, it's about the future. If you cannot strike a deal by October, Britain will be out by June next year. But remember, a 'no deal' isn't in our favour."

Williamson nodded, carefully absorbing the gravitas of the prime minister's words.

Field Marshal Claud Bernard, with his military cap perched beside him, chimed in, "The real treasure, gentlemen, isn't the land but the strategic advantage India provides. The war has shown us the importance of India's manpower. Two million Indian soldiers were our strength at our weakest point. It's not just manpower; it's the naval bases, the ports, the potential war supplies. And don't get me started on the significance of oil supplies from Persia."

Atlee's gaze was unwavering. "Go on, Claud."

Bernard continued, "Now is the time to fragment India, gentlemen. A northwest region, under a new state—Pakistan—could remain our strategic ally. Their bases and ports would be indispensable to the Commonwealth. And if we play our cards right, we can ensure its effective civil administration by embedding our advisors."

Williamson, trying to piece together the puzzle, interjected, "I'm struggling to see the larger picture, gentlemen. Are we merely concerned about military strategy?"

Atlee, exhaling deeply, spoke gravely, "William, our empire has weathered the greatest war in history. We can't have a powerful, united India challenging our global dominance. A divided subcontinent is easier to control and manipulate. Plus, if India becomes socialist or aligns with the Soviets, it's a direct threat to us. An independent Pakistan will be a buffer, a friend in the East."

Williamson, realizing the depth of the empire's vision, nodded. "So, the play isn't just about India. It's about the larger geopolitical stage. The Soviets, the oil, the Commonwealth."

Bernard leaned back. "Precisely. And if we can pull this off, we'd have secured our interests for decades to come."

Cyrus reemerged from the depths of the story that had held the room captive, the silence lingering like a solemn note sustained beyond the close of a symphony. Time itself seemed to pause, caught between the revelations of yesteryears and the pressing pulse of the present.

He observed the space around him, each individual encapsulated in their own cocoon of contemplation. Bernard's narrative had waned, leaving in its wake a subdued aura of contemplation.

Breaking the long silence, Bernard continued. "The empire had its motives, and they feared a united Indian subcontinent, especially one that might lean towards socialism, or worse, align with the Soviets."

Cyrus interjected, "But we gained our independence. We're not bound by their machinations anymore."

Bernard explained, "Indeed, but remnants of their network remain. There are Indian spies, placed during the Raj, who still report to British handlers. Their main goal? Keeping India and Russia apart."

Cyrus's eyes darkened. The implications of what he was hearing were monumental. Not only was he navigating the challenges of a newly independent nation, but the shadows of the past still loomed large. The great game, it seemed, was far from over.

Cyrus sunk deep into thought. After a while, he asked, "So, you're saying the current spy situation is a continuation of a strategy set in motion years ago?"

Bernard sighed. "Yes, but it's also possible that certain elements, even within the British establishment, have acted on their own, deviating from the original intentions."

Cyrus nodded, absorbing the seriousness of the revelations. "Then, Field Marshal Bernard, our work is cut out. It's time to untangle this web and discover the truth hidden within its threads. Thank you for your time."

"Send Nalini, to my office immediately." Cyrus's voice came through firm and urgent.

"Certainly," replied Mr. Nair.

Brushing aside her discomfort from the heat, Nalini hurriedly made her way to the prime minister's chambers. Cyrus stood with his back to the door, gazing out over the sprawling gardens.

As Nalini entered, Cyrus began without preamble, "Our past with the British Raj has left deep-rooted traces, Nalini. Not just in our bureaucracy and railroads but deeper, more covert remnants. They've embedded a spy network deep within Soviet territories."

Nalini's eyebrows shot up. Whispers and speculations had always circled these topics, but a direct acknowledgement was unexpected.

Cyrus turned to face Nalini, his eyes grave. "Several of our own were sent as spies into Soviet territories during the Raj. Many are still operational, providing intel to the old British intelligence channels. We must put an end to this."

Taking a moment to process the information, Nalini finally responded, "Sir, you mean to—"

Cyrus cut her off. "Yes. We need to dismantle this network and bring our people back. It's time they come home. Coordinate a high-level meeting with our Russian counterparts. It's paramount."

"Cyrus, dismantling an entire spy network in Russia is no small feat. The British Raj's tentacles run deep there," Nalini warned, her voice heavy with concern.

Cyrus leaned forward, determination evident in his eyes. "We've inherited this network, but we aren't bound by its past. India is taking a different path, Nalini, and we cannot harbour spies in an allied nation. It's time to cleanse the legacy."

Nalini nodded, understanding the significance of the task ahead. "It begins with the embassy. We'll have to discreetly interview every staff member."

The operation was christened 'Operation Snowfall'. Within days, the Indian embassy in Moscow was buzzing with discreet activity. Officials were pulled into closed-door meetings, files were revisited, and communications intercepted. Nalini's team worked in shifts, scanning every piece of outgoing and incoming information. Each day was a tightrope walk, maintaining a diplomatic façade while conducting a covert internal investigation.

Parallelly, in India, a specialized team hunted down contacts of the sleeper cells. Dark alleys, secret rendezvous points, and covert communications hubs were discovered and discreetly monitored. Every person with ties to the spy network was meticulously tracked, with some being taken into custody under the cover of darkness.

The intelligence suggested the existence of 'The Whisperer', a mastermind who had been the British Raj's eyes and ears within the Soviet Union. The search for this enigmatic figure became the linchpin of the operation.

Back in Moscow, the noose tightened. Undercover agents posed as diplomats, clerks, and even janitors, working tirelessly to trace the tendrils of the espionage web. Secrets, once confined to the shadows, now emerged into the stark light of day.

A pivotal moment came when an embassy clerk, shaken by the scrutiny, sought asylum in the Soviet Union, exposing key figures in the process. This revelation was the catalyst that led to the identification and eventual extraction of 'The Whisperer' — a high-ranking embassy official whose double life was a shock to both nations.

By the end of 1950, Operation Snowfall saw the dismantling of one of the most intricate spy networks of its time. It was a demonstration of India's commitment to its allies and a signal to the world that the nation was carving its own path, free from the shadows of its colonial past. India, under Cyrus's leadership, was striving for transparency and integrity on the global stage.

Chapter 9

GAME OF CHESS

August 10, 1952: New Delhi

As the heart of the nation pulsed with excitement, the capital was draped in a riot of colours as the celebrated its fifth Independence Day. Tricolour flags fluttered everywhere, from government buildings to roadside stalls, making a profound statement of unity. The entire city seemed to have taken on a festive hue, with lanterns illuminating the streets and the sweet melodies of patriotic songs wafting through the air. Residents, regardless of age or status, were busy adding their touches to the grand celebration, be it through arranging cultural programs or simply decorating their homes.

India Gate, an iconic symbol of the city, was the centre of attention. Skilled craftsmen and workers laboured day and night, erecting a grand stage where Prime Minister Engineer would address the nation. Rows upon rows of chairs were set up for dignitaries and the general public while a separate dais was being prepared for cultural performances. Flower vendors made their way there, their baskets overflowing with marigolds and roses, ready to be strung into garlands that would adorn the monument.

School children, dressed in crisp uniforms, practised their march-past on Rajpath, their shoes clicking rhythmically against the tarred road. They shouldered the legacy of the past and the promise of the future, representing a young and vibrant India.

While the atmosphere was jubilant, security was also tighter than ever. Men in khaki patrolled every nook and corner to ensure that the celebrations went off without a hitch. The excitement was intense, and a sense of national pride filled the air.

The radio stations and newspapers had been abuzz for days with the news that Clairant Atlee would be attending the Independence Day celebrations as a special guest. It wasn't just any visit; it held historical significance. The presence of the prime minister of the United Kingdom marked a profound gesture of reconciliation and friendship. He was accompanied by Lord Williamson and his entourage of diplomats and businessmen. His visit marked the first official bilateral meeting post-independence. While many were still grappling with the scars of the past, the joint presence of the two leaders was a testament to the spirit of diplomacy, collaboration, and the forging of a new relationship between two sovereign nations.

The meticulously curated events of the day had the dual purpose of reflecting on past struggles and looking forward to the promise of a brighter, shared future. To see Lord Williamson, the man who once held such influence over India's destiny, now sitting side by side with Indian leaders was symbolic of the shift in dynamics. The world was watching, and New Bharat was ready to show that it held no grudges, but instead, sought peace, growth, and mutual respect with all nations.

The stage was set for a historic 15th of August, where the past and future would converge, marking an indelible moment in the annals of New Bharat's history.

In the midst of these bustling preparations, a sharp contrast was presented at the prime minister's office. The sprawling room, usually filled with the buzz of activity, was unusually quiet. Cyrus sat behind his desk, scanning through the endless documents and making last-minute checks for the upcoming event with Nair and Nalini.

Nair, was busy taking notes on a parchment, jotting down points about the upcoming events. He looked up as Cyrus's eyes met his. "Cyrus, we've made sure that every state will have its own representative attending the ceremony. It'll showcase our unity in diversity, the very ethos of our new Bharat," he said with a hint of pride.

Nalini's face broke into a rare smile. "It's imperative that our citizens see this. They need to know that their leaders stand united, irrespective of our personal beliefs."

Suddenly, the silence was disrupted by a knock. Mrs. Chatterjee, hurriedly entered, holding a sealed envelope with a sense of urgency.

"Sir, a telegram," she announced, her voice reflecting the importance of its contents.

The room was filled with tense anticipation as Cyrus carefully unfolded the telegram and began to read. His face, usually composed, showed hints of surprise, and then concern.

She looked up, her eyes scanning the room. "It's from Ali Bhai."

Cyrus hesitated for a moment, then read out the contents of the telegram.

To Hon. Prime Minister Cyrus Engineer,

Your actions today have confirmed my greatest fears. I always championed for a united India, where a minority could hold power, not to be suppressed by the majority. But the recent events make me question the foundation of this democracy.

Moving to London with family for the foreseeable future. I entrust my homeland to you, hoping that my fears remain unfounded.

Lastly, seek some answers from Panditji and Patel Sahib on the settlement terms.

Best, Ali Bhai.

As he finished, an uneasy silence fell over the room, interrupted only by the distant sounds of a bustling New Delhi outside.

Nalini finally spoke. "This is serious, Mr. Prime Minister. Ali Bhai's departure will create a political storm."

Cyrus nodded. "I'm aware, Nalini. But what concerns me more is the mention of a settlement. What is this arrangement he speaks of with Patel Sahib and Panditji?"

The spacious office of the prime minister was silent, save for the soft humming of the ceiling fan above. Cyrus sat tense behind his desk, the telegram from Ali Bhai spread out in front of him.

He read and reread the telegram, the words echoing in his mind. What 'settlement' was Ali Bhai talking about? A cold feeling of dread settled in his stomach.

"Nair!" he called out.

Nair, concern evident in his eyes, asked, "Yes, Mr. Prime Minister?"

"Arrange a meeting with Panditji and Patel Sahib. Now."

"But, sir, it's almost late evening."

"I don't care. This can't wait," Cyrus replied, the urgency evident in his voice.

Nair nodded, understanding the gravity of the situation. "Very well, sir. I'll see to it immediately."

Cyrus leaned back in his chair, massaging his temples. He felt trapped in a complex web of political intrigue, and he desperately needed answers. What had he been thrust into, and what secrets lay hidden in the corridors of power?

Time seemed to slow down as he waited. But eventually, the sounds of hushed voices and hurried footsteps approached. The door swung open, revealing the silhouettes of Panditji and Patel Sahib.

Panditji, as usual, was the first to speak, his voice heavy. "Cyrus, what's so urgent?"

Handing over the telegram to both, Cyrus's eyes searched theirs for answers. "What is this 'settlement' Ali Bhai speaks of?"

The two stalwarts exchanged a glance, an unspoken understanding passing between them. This was a moment that would define the path forward for the trio, and perhaps, the entire nation.

"Cyrus," Panditji began, "the seeds of this planning were sown long before you assumed office. You've only seen the tip of the iceberg."

Panditji sighed deeply, a heaviness evident in his eyes. "Let me take you back, Cyrus, to a day that changed the fate of this great nation."

The room seemed to darken a touch, as if clouds had passed overhead, as Panditji began his tale.

"It was the third of June 1947. The room was thick with tension. Lord Williamson, the last governor general of India, had called a meeting. Ali Bhai, Patel Sahib, Shaukat, and I were present. Each one of us is aware of the magnitude of our decisions."

The flashback transported Cyrus to a grand room, with heavy wooden doors at its entrance and a massive table around which sat the leaders.

June 3, 1947: The Governor General's House

Lord Williamson, tall, and imperious in his demeanour, took the lead. "Gentlemen, the British Empire has seen its best days. It's evident that India must be given its freedom. But the question is, how?"

Ali Bhai interjected, "Our people demand a separate land, a home for Muslims. We cannot be sidelined anymore!"

Patel, with a stern face, retorted, "India has lived in unity for centuries. Dividing based on religion will lead to unimaginable consequences."

Shaukat, trying to mediate, suggested, "The division might be the only way to avoid a large-scale civil war."

Panditji's voice brought a sense of reason to the room. "Partitioning the land is one thing. But what about the hearts and souls of the people? How can you draw lines there?"

Lord Williamson, sensing the escalating tension, declared, "Gentlemen, it seems we are at an impasse. But we need a solution, and quickly."

As the scene of the past unfurled, listeners around Cyrus were transported, the room transforming into a vessel sailing through time, buoyed by the undercurrents of his narrative.

Patel Sahib then took over from Panditji and continued, "The discussion went on for hours. Tempers flared, alliances were tested, and at times, it felt like the room would explode. But amid all that chaos, one thing became clear. We needed a leader who would be impartial, one who stood beyond the divides of religion."

Cyrus, engrossed in the narrative, realized where this was heading. "And that's when my name was proposed?"

Panditji nodded. "Yes. You were neither a Hindu nor a Muslim, but a Parsi. Your father, a renowned philanthropist, had the respect of both communities. You were seen as a bridge, a beacon of hope in those turbulent times." Cyrus's patience was wearing thin. He had been listening to Patel Sahib and Panditji recount details and events, most of which he was already well-acquainted with. His fingers tapped a restless rhythm on the desk, his gaze shifting between the two men as they spoke. "Gentlemen," he stated, his voice tinged with a barely controlled frustration, "I am well aware of the history and the events that led us here. What I need to understand now are the specifics of this so-called 'settlement' that Ali Bhai referred to in his telegram. What exactly was agreed upon? What were the terms?"

Patel Sahib exchanged a quick, hesitant glance with Panditji before responding. "Cyrus, we assure you that the decisions made were in the best interest of our nation's future. We had to consider the delicate balance of power, the potential for civil unrest…"

Cyrus cut him off. "I appreciate that, Patel Sahib, but those are broad strokes. I need details. Ali Bhai's message implied that there were specific terms agreed upon, terms that I am not privy to. This lack of transparency is what concerns me."

"That day," Patel Sahib continued, "when we thought the lines of division were set in stone, when Ali Bhai was about to push India down the path of partition, something extraordinary happened."

Patel Sahib paused, gathering his thoughts. "Ali Bhai began to cough violently during the discussion. He pulled out his handkerchief, and when he removed it from his mouth, it was soaked with blood."

Cyrus felt a cold shock.

Patel Sahib cleared his throat, shifting uneasily. "Cyrus, the matter is more intricate than it seems. Ali Bhai's telegram refers to a series of discussions, agreements, and perhaps, some compromises that were made during the tumultuous days leading up to our independence. But to give you the complete picture, Lord Williamson must be present. He was instrumental in the entire process."

Cyrus's eyes darkened, his gaze piercing. "Why am I hearing about this only now? Why was I kept in the dark?"

Panditji, interjected, "Cyrus, we did not want to burden you with these intricacies at the outset. It was a volatile time, and certain decisions had to be made quickly."

"And behind closed doors," Cyrus added bitterly.

Patel Sahib nodded sombrely. "Sometimes, for the greater good, transparency becomes a luxury. But you have every right to know."

Cyrus's gaze shifted between Panditji and Patel Sahib, a silent war of trust and betrayal raging within him. "Nair, please summon Lord Williamson immediately."

Nair, sensing the tension in the room, hurried out without a word.

An hour later, the majestic car of Lord Williamson pulled up to the entrance of the prime minister's residence. As the British diplomat stepped out, he was met with the stern faces of India's leaders.

As he was ushered into Cyrus's office, Williamson greeted him with a light-hearted remark. "Cyrus, you've summoned me quite early. There's still time before the Independence Day parade begins. Is there a new float you want me to review?"

Cyrus, however, did not reciprocate Williamson's jovial mood. His expression was stern, a stark contrast to the light-heartedness of Williamson's comment. Without a word, he extended his hand, passing a single piece of paper to Williamson. It was the telegram sent by Ali Bhai, laden with implications that had sent ripples through the highest echelons of government.

Williamson's smile faded as he took the telegram, his eyes quickly scanning the contents. The atmosphere in the room shifted palpably. The seriousness of Cyrus's demeanour was unmistakable.

Cyrus broke the silence, his voice firm and demanding. "Lord Williamson, I need answers. This telegram from Ali Bhai raises questions that cannot be ignored. I expect a full explanation."

The reunion was cold and tense. The room, heavy with the yoke of secrets, witnessed the four men, architects of a nascent nation, come face to face with the unspoken truths of the past.

"This telegram from Mr. Ali Bhai suggests there's more to the story of the partition's abandonment than we've been led to believe. How does a man let go of a dream he's harboured and nurtured for years, and that too, overnight?"

Cyrus's gaze was unwavering, boring into Lord Williamson, who sat opposite him, the impact of Cyrus's words hanging between them. "This is not just a matter of curiosity," Cyrus continued, "it's a matter that could impact the very fabric of our diplomatic relations. I warn you, it's in your best interest to come clean now. A diplomatic standoff is the last thing we need. Rest assured, this conversation remains within these walls. But it's crucial that we understand the past to navigate our future more effectively."

Lord Williamson, usually composed and articulate, seemed to grapple with the situation, understanding the severity of Cyrus's warning. "Prime Minister," he began, choosing his words with care, "the decision to forego partition was not made lightly. There were numerous factors at play, factors that extended beyond the immediate political landscape."

Cyrus leaned forward, his eyes fixed on Lord Williamson. "I understand the complexity of the situation, but what I seek is transparency. Mr. Ali Bhai's sudden change of heart raises questions, questions that deserve answers." Williamson, his disposition calm but eyes betraying a hint of apprehension, met Cyrus's gaze. "Indeed, Mr. Prime Minister. There are tales from the corridors of power that perhaps now you should be privy to."

Williamson, leaning against the mahogany table, let out a sigh. He looked deep into Cyrus's eyes, seemingly weighing whether or not to reveal a well-guarded secret.

"Before the crucial meet on the third of June, 1947, there was an encounter. One that hasn't been spoken of, until now," began Williamson, his voice a low murmur.

As he narrated the clandestine meeting with Ali Bhai, Cyrus felt as if he were being transported back in time, witnessing the delicate dance of power, promises, and politics.

June 2, 1947: Ali Bhai's Residence, Bombay

The room was awash with the pale hues of morning light, flickering shadows playing across the mahogany walls. Williamson, in a crisply ironed suit, felt out of place in the warmly lit, traditional interior of Ali Bhai's residence. It was a tangible manifestation of the divide between them.

The atmosphere was tense as the two men faced each other.

"Good morning, Ali Bhai," Williamson greeted, taking in his surroundings.

Ali Bhai, although taken aback by the unannounced visit, kept his composure. "Good morning, William. Your sudden appearance suggests something urgent."

"Preparation is key, especially when the stakes are this high," Williamson retorted, his voice smooth yet assertive.

Ali Bhai gestured to the plush sofa. "Please, sit. Perhaps some tea?"

Williamson nodded. "No sugar, thank you."

As the servant moved to prepare the tea, Ali Bhai enquired, "So, to what do I owe this surprise?"

"Your partition demands," began Williamson, "are causing ripples, Ali Bhai. You know very well that some of these demands won't sit well with Panditji."

Ali Bhai's expression darkened. "Your empire has always decided for us. Isn't it only fair that we decide for ourselves now?"

Williamson sighed, realizing the depth of the sentiment. "Your request for the eight-hundred-mile-long corridor is seen between East Pakistan and West Pakistan as a strategic play, one that Panditji believes won't come to fruition."

Ali Bhai was unyielding. "It's vital for Pakistan's survival. And it's a fair ask."

As Williamson sipped his tea, he decided to lay his cards on the table. "My prime minister believes you're an enigma, Ali Bhai. Previous experiences suggest you enjoy keeping everyone guessing."

A slight smirk played on Ali Bhai's lips. "Go on."

"How about a deal? You support our proposal in the upcoming meeting, and in return, we ensure the princely states of Kashmir, Hyderabad, and Junagarh accede to Pakistan. I only ask one thing: when I state that you've provided assurances, you don't contradict me."

Ali Bhai's eyes gleamed with a mixture of amusement and anger. "A puppet's role doesn't appeal to me."

As Williamson rose to leave, he paused, his silhouette framed by the window. "Ali Bhai, my goal is a peaceful settlement. I hope you won't stand in its way."

Ali Bhai watched him go, a storm of thoughts raging in his mind. The game of politics was afoot, and the board was set.

Cyrus, with his sharp journalist instincts, sensed there was something Williamson hadn't disclosed yet. "Mr. Williamson," he began, "you seem to be privy to more than what meets the eye regarding Ali Bhai's sudden change of stance. There's a subtext to this narrative, isn't there?"

Panditji, intrigued, leaned forward. "Go on."

Taking a deep breath, Williamson began, "He was acutely aware of his deteriorating health. He knew he wouldn't live long enough to see the aftermath of the partition. What weighed on him was the legacy he would leave behind."

"Seeing his own life hanging by a thread, Ali Bhai had an epiphany. He looked at me, his eyes filled with pain and realization. 'I cannot,' he whispered hoarsely, 'tear apart a nation when I myself am falling apart.' The reality of his imminent mortality made him see the broader picture, the irreparable damage that partition would cause. He voiced his concerns, stating that with his condition, he didn't want to leave behind a legacy of division and bloodshed."

Cyrus interjected, "Are you suggesting that his decision to reconsider the division was influenced by his knowledge of his impending end?"

Williamson nodded. "Precisely. He was deeply troubled by the thought of a newborn nation plunged into leaderless chaos. He believed that without him at the helm, Pakistan would be at the mercy of power struggles, with potential civil wars and unrest."

Panditji's face was shadowed with realization. "So, he felt trapped. He was a pawn in this grand game of chess, with the British Empire calling the shots. And he realized that, perhaps, his greatest move would be not to move at all."

Lord Williamson, with a hint of unease, began to unravel the hidden narrative. "Gentlemen, when I proposed the idea of Pakistan, I thought Ali Bhai would be the pawn in our larger game. The creation of Pakistan was intended to limit India's influence and curb its tilt towards the Soviets," he confessed, his voice tinged with a mixture of regret and realization.

"However," Williamson continued, "Ali Bhai played a double game. He agreed to the plan of a united India but on one critical condition—the appointment of a novice as prime minister. And with Hamid controlling the major decisions, Ali Bhai attempted to position himself as the ultimate kingmaker."

Cyrus's expression hardened as the implications of Williamson's revelations sank in. The political landscape he had navigated was even more treacherous than he had realized. Ali Bhai, whom he had seen as a key figure in preventing the partition, had his own agenda, manipulating the situation to emerge as a power broker in the newly united India.

Williamson, noticing Cyrus's contemplative silence, added, "I underestimated Ali Bhai. He wasn't just a mere participant in our plans. He was playing a far deeper game, ensuring that he remained a pivotal figure in the political equation, irrespective of the outcome." After a brief pause, Williamson continued, "He envisioned a united India as a strong counter to the British Empire. He knew that division would weaken both nations. But he also understood the allure of power and the looming threats of civil war if he was no longer around."

Patel Sahib interrupted, "But why didn't he disclose this meeting to the leadership the very next day?"

Williamson smiled wryly. "Ah, that's where the true complexity of Ali Bhai's nature comes in. He saw the larger geopolitical game at play. He understood the British intentions, the looming Cold War, and how India could become a pawn in this larger game. He wanted to ensure that no matter what, India remained united."

Cyrus interjected, his voice edged with scepticism, "And how would he ensure that? By striking a secret deal with the departing colonial masters?"

Williamson continued, "Not quite. His proposal was simple. He would use his influence, his resources, and his connections to ensure India did not bleed due to partition. But in return, he wanted assurances—assurances that the interests of the minority, which he represented, would not be trampled upon in the newly independent nation. His trump card was Hamid."

Cyrus, his thoughts a whirlpool of emotions, realized the enormity of the situation. "And what of Hamid's role in all this?" he asked, seeking to understand the full extent of the political chess game he was unwittingly a part of.

"Hamid was Ali Bhai's ace," Williamson replied. "His appointment was a strategic move to ensure that Ali Bhai's influence lingered, even without direct involvement. Hamid's recent actions, however, seem to indicate that he might be playing his own game now."

Panditji took a deep breath, his eyes distant but sharp. "Hamid's appointment as the finance minister wasn't straightforward, you see. Shaukat, being the astute political player he is, had ambitions for his son."

Cyrus shifted in his seat, leaning forward. "So, Hamid was a compromise?"

"In a way, yes," Panditji replied. "Ali Bhai's initial insistence was that if India was to be undivided, the

Muslim Quam would want representation in the highest echelons of power. He desired Shaukat's son to be a part of the cabinet."

"But why finance? That's a pivotal role, especially for a new nation," Cyrus interjected, his brows furrowed.

Panditji smiled, a hint of melancholy in his eyes. "Indeed, it is. But see, Shaukat and many in his camp were wary of giving the second most significant portfolio to a Hindu. It was a matter of pride and assertion. As finance minister of a new nation, Hamid had such extraordinary powers, which sometimes even undermined the office of the prime minister."

Cyrus thought back to his meetings with Patel. "But things changed after the earthquake, didn't they?"

Panditji nodded. "They did. Patel's suggestion to involve Gokhale and the RSD in relief work was, in many ways, a masterstroke. It showcased a spirit of unity and capability. And when the time came for deciding on the home minister, the scales tilted in Gokhale's favour."

The atmosphere in the room grew tense. The soft chink of ice in Cyrus's glass as he took a sip from his drink was the only sound breaking the heavy silence.

"I still find it hard to believe," Cyrus murmured. "All these backdoor discussions, the balancing act.

It's almost like a grand game of chess, with India as the board." Cyrus leaned back, his mind racing with the newfound knowledge of the political intrigue that had shaped his rise to power. "So, the chessboard was set with players I was barely aware of," he mused aloud. "And all this while, I thought I was making independent decisions, unaware of the deeper currents that were influencing the very foundation of our nation."

Williamson nodded, a hint of admiration in his tone. "Cyrus, you were thrust into a game much larger than you realized. But it's also a testament to your leadership that you've navigated these turbulent waters with such adeptness."

Panditji chuckled. "That's politics for you, my dear Cyrus. But remember, while the game might be intricate, the end goal is clear—a prosperous and united India."

Cyrus looked thoughtful. "So, in essence, Ali Bhai tried to avoid partition by ensuring rights for the minority by giving the second-most important portfolio in the cabinet to Muslim? It doesn't sound noble on the surface."

Panditji sighed. "But in the end, did his actions not benefit India? We remained united, and the bloodshed was minimized. Should we not judge him by the results of his actions rather than the intentions behind them?"

Williamson nodded in agreement. "The game of chess has many players—pawns, bishops, and queens. But in the end, it's the moves you make that define the game. Ali Bhai, for better or worse, played his moves. Now, history will judge him."

Cyrus sighed. "It's a tragedy. A leader's personal dilemma intertwined with the fate of millions. How the personal becomes political."

The room fell silent, each person lost in thought. Outside, the sun dipped below the horizon, casting long shadows that seemed to reflect the complexities of the decisions made within those walls.

Cyrus looked at Williamson, realizing the intricate machinations that had shaped their nation. The past, it seemed, was never truly behind them. After the tale was told, a profound silence engulfed the room. Cyrus was visibly moved. "So much happens behind the curtains. Choices, sacrifices, compromises…"

Williamson nodded. "Yes, it's a complex maze, and often the narrative woven for the public is but a fraction of the entire story."

Cyrus leaned back, processing everything. "And here I thought I knew everything that went behind the curtain. It's a learning curve every day."

The two shared a glance, the future of the nation hanging in balance as they navigated the political maze.

The dynamics between Ali Bhai, the British, and the Indian leadership revealed the multifaceted nature of political leadership. It raised pressing questions about the true essence of sacrifice, the motivations behind actions, and the complex interplay of power.

As the sun cast its first rays on a new day, the leaders were left to grapple with this new understanding. The story of India's independence, it seemed, was not just black and white but painted with shades of grey. And at the centre of it all was Ali Bhai, a figure whose legacy, be it of a master strategist or a community leader, would be dissected and discussed for generations to come.

Chapter 10

CHECKMATE

November 13, 1952:
The Prime Minister's Office

There was a sense of anxious expectation in the prime minister's office. The walls, lined with portraits of past leaders and adorned with ornate Indian artwork, bore silent witness to the momentous meetings these walls had seen over the past years.

Dr. Dharmadhikari, holding a thick sheaf of papers, took long strides into the room. His face showed visible signs of exhaustion, and yet his eyes sparkled with pride. He had spent the better part of three years on this document, consulting, debating, and at times, even pacifying vehement opposition from different quarters. It was an arduous task, taking into account the complexities of India's diverse population, yet he was determined to produce a constitution that would stand the test of time.

Cyrus, noticing the confident gleam in Dr. Dharmadhikari's eyes, stood up and extended his hand. "It's done then?"

Dr. Dharmadhikari, placing the papers on the grand teak table, nodded. "Yes, Mr. Prime Minister.

This is our Constitution. The very backbone of our democracy."

Gokhale, always meticulous, began leafing through the pages. He stopped abruptly when his eyes landed on the preamble, reading aloud, "… to secure to all its citizens: JUSTICE, social, economic, and political; LIBERTY of thought, expression, belief, faith, and worship; EQUALITY of status and of opportunity; and to promote among them all FRATERNITY, assuring the dignity of the individual and the unity and integrity of the Nation; IN OUR CONSTITUENT ASSEMBLY this 26th day of November, 1952, we do HEREBY ADOPT, ENACT, AND GIVE TO OURSELVES THIS CONSTITUTION."

He paused, took a deep breath, and continued, "We, the people of India, having solemnly resolved to constitute India into a SOVEREIGN **SECULAR** DEMOCRATIC REPUBLIC—"

Gokhale looked up sharply, locking his eyes on Dharmadhikari. "Secular? We never agreed to this term."

Cyrus interjected calmly, "Gokhaleji, the idea is to ensure every citizen, regardless of their faith, feels equally represented and protected."

Dharmadhikari nodded. "Exactly, Mr. Prime Minister. The word 'secular' doesn't mean the state is against religion. It simply assures no religion will be given preference over another."

Gokhale, visibly upset, responded, "But why now? Why wasn't this discussed with the broader team?"

Cyrus took a deep breath. "It was a last-minute addition, reflecting the feedback from various stakeholders. A reminder of the need for our country to stay neutral in matters of faith."

Silence enveloped the room. The enormity of the decision rested heavily on the shoulders of the three men.

Finally, Gokhale spoke, "I understand the sentiment, but we should've been consulted. This will have repercussions."

Cyrus nodded, understandingly. "I respect your sentiment, Gokhaleji. But we must stand by this decision for the betterment of our nation."

Dharmadhikari, looking at the two leaders, added, "It's done. We've crafted this with diligence and care. We must now present it to the people of India."

The air was thick with tension as Gokhale and Cyrus stood facing each other. Two titans of their era, both driven by the love of their nation but with starkly different visions of its future. It was late, shadows thrown by a single lamplight dancing on the walls, and outside, the distant sounds of a bustling New Delhi could still be heard.

Cyrus, his voice edged with frustration, began, "Gokhaleji, I respect your principles, and I understand your vision for a Hindu Rashtra. But India is not just Hindu. We've built this nation on the principles of secularism, diversity, and unity."

Gokhale's eyes, always intense, now bore into Cyrus. "Cyrus, don't mistake my intentions. I'm not advocating for the exclusion of others. My vision for a Hindu Rashtra is one where Hindu culture, which is inherently inclusive, forms the backbone of our great nation."

Cyrus took a deep breath. "I've seen the passion of your cadres. Their dedication during the Bombay rebuilding was admirable. But don't you see? They were not just helping Hindus. They were helping everyone. Isn't that the true essence of India?"

Gokhale countered, "That's exactly my point. The very essence of Hinduism is universal brotherhood. I'm not talking about a theocratic state. I'm envisioning a nation where our deep-rooted ethos, which has always welcomed everyone, shines through."

Cyrus hesitated for a moment, then said, "But forcing a singular identity… doesn't it undermine the rich history of diverse cultures, beliefs, and traditions that make India unique?"

"The ethos of this land has been Hindu for millennia," Gokhale began, his voice reflecting years of wisdom. "It's not just a religion; it's our culture, our civilization, our very identity. The idea of Hinduism is rooted in secular principles. Every individual has a right to pursue their path to divinity, and that's what makes us unique."

Cyrus, taking a deep breath, responded, "While I respect your sentiments, Gokhaleji, this is a new dawn for India. While our roots may be Hindu, our branches have been nourished by many faiths. It's crucial for our democracy that we don't prioritize one religion over the other."

"But, Cyrus," Gokhale interjected, "calling India 'Hindu' does not marginalize other religions. It merely acknowledges the majority and the rich history that is interwoven with its essence."

Cyrus leaned forward. "You see, Gokhaleji, the danger is not in the term but in its potential misuse. In the hands of those with divisive intentions, it might be wielded as a weapon."

Gokhale, a staunch proponent of recognizing India's Hindu majority, began by grounding his arguments in historical and cultural perspectives. "Cyrus," he began with a measured tone, "from the Vedic texts to the grandeur of the Mauryan and Gupta empires, our history has been deeply intertwined with Hinduism. And it's not merely about worship but a way of life, a philosophy, a guideline for righteousness."

Cyrus, never one to be outdone, responded, "Gokhaleji, I respect our shared history, but our future must be built on the principle of inclusion. A land where every faith, every belief, finds equal footing."

The room was charged with anticipation. Both stalwarts hung on to every word, understanding the magnitude of what was being decided.

Gokhale, tapping the constitution draft, said, "This document will shape the identity of our nation. It's only right that we recognize Hinduism's vast contributions. After all, the ethos of dharma, karma, and yoga are fundamentally secular in nature, allowing for a myriad of beliefs and practices."

Cyrus countered, "Yet, Gokhaleji, by overtly favouring Hinduism, we risk overshadowing the countless contributions of Sikhs, Jains, Buddhists, Christians, Muslims, and innumerable others who have called this land home. We risk alienating them and fostering resentment."

Gokhale's face showed a hint of frustration. "It's not about overshadowing, Cyrus. It's about acknowledging the predominant culture while ensuring that others flourish. It's about embracing our identity as a predominantly Hindu nation while ensuring that other faiths are respected and protected."

"However," Cyrus quickly interjected, "by labelling India as a 'Hindu nation', we inadvertently set a precedent that can be misinterpreted and misused in the future. Secularism is not just a word, it's an ideal. An ideal that promises every Indian, irrespective of their faith, equal rights and protections."

The debate continued with Gokhale emphasizing that Hinduism itself was the epitome of secularism. "Look at our festivals, our scriptures, our traditions. They don't just accommodate diversity, they celebrate it. Why then is it wrong to want our nation's identity to reflect that?"

Cyrus, sipping on his water, responded, "Because, Gokhaleji, while the principles of Hinduism might be secular, the political interpretation of those principles might not be. Today, we might be sitting here with the best intentions, but what of those who come after us? How can we ensure that this 'Hindu' label won't be used as a tool for exclusion?"

Gokhale leaned in. "But isn't that true for any word, any principle? Any ideal can be misinterpreted. Does that mean we live in fear and avoid stating facts?"

Cyrus nodded thoughtfully. "That's precisely why our Constitution must be clear, unambiguous. It should leave no room for misinterpretation. By explicitly endorsing secularism, we make a promise to every citizen, now and in the future, that they belong."

The debate continued for what seemed like hours, neither yielding, each point met with a counterpoint, each argument with a rebuttal. The room became a battleground of ideologies.

Finally, Gokhale, his voice tinged with sadness and perhaps a hint of resignation, said, "I've dedicated my life to this nation. And I believe, genuinely believe, in what I advocate. But if the path I see for our nation isn't the one you envision, then perhaps it's best I step away. Our visions for India are diverging. I can't continue like this."

Cyrus frowned, taking a moment to process the unexpected revelation. "Are we talking about just one issue, or is there something deeper?"

Gokhale sighed heavily. "I believe our fundamental visions for India's future are no longer aligned."

Cyrus rose from his desk, pacing the floor, a storm of emotions evident in his eyes. "So, what are you saying, Gokhale?"

Taking a deep breath, Gokhale uttered the words he had been dreading, "I am tendering my resignation."

Cyrus stopped, disbelief clouding his face. "Just because of one word?"

"Cyrus," Gokhale continued, "while your leadership in uniting the country is commendable, there have been instances where your approach has been, let's say, too diplomatic. Take the issue of Palestine, for instance."

Cyrus stiffened, his expression turning wary. He had known that the topic would come up eventually, but he had hoped for a different setting.

Gokhale continued, "Your stance, or rather lack of it, regarding the Palestine conflict hasn't gone unnoticed. By trying to play it safe, by attempting to placate all sides, you've inadvertently shown a lack of decisive leadership."

The room's atmosphere grew even more charged.

Gokhale took a step closer to the centre of the room, addressing Cyrus. "It's not just about secularism, nor is it about pleasing one community over the other. It's about making tough choices, standing by them, and leading the nation through its ramifications. And on the issue of Palestine, we failed."

Cyrus met Gokhale's gaze, fully absorbing the implications of his words. "I understand the sentiment, Gokhale," he began slowly, "but these decisions aren't made in isolation. They are a result of numerous discussions, debates, and considerations."

Gokhale sighed. "I respect the deliberative process, Cyrus. But sometimes, a leader must take a firm stand, even if it's unpopular. That's what defines true leadership. Our approaches towards a particular issue aren't differences anymore. They've become divides. And I think it's best for both of us, and for India, if I step aside."

The room fell into an oppressive silence. The air was thick with the irreversible nature of Gokhale's decision. The wall clock's ticking seemed unbearably loud in the quiet.

Cyrus's voice, when he finally spoke, was hoarse. "This was never just about the two of us. It was about the dream of a united, prosperous India. Are you really willing to walk away from that?"

Gokhale's eyes shimmered with unshed tears. "I still believe in that dream, Cyrus. But maybe it's time for a different path to achieve it."

As the confrontation between Gokhale and Cyrus drew to a close, Mr. Nair, always one to defuse tension, interjected, "Gentlemen, if I may. Sometimes, when two bulls lock horns, it's the grass that suffers. And right now, that grass is looking pretty trampled!" Both men paused and then shared a brief, tension-cutting smirk.

Gokhale moved to leave. Cyrus, suddenly overcome with emotion and respect for the man in front of him, took a step forward and tried to touch Gokhale's feet for blessings.

Gokhale stopped him, a gentle smile on his face. "See, Cyrus, this... this is the Hindu ethos I talk about. You, a Parsi, trying to touch my feet, following a tradition so deeply rooted in Hinduism. It's not about religion but about respect, values, and traditions."

Cyrus looked up, eyes glistening, and Gokhale continued, "This respect for elders, for traditions, for values—this is the India I dream of. An India where its ethos shines irrespective of the religion one follows."

The evening had surrendered to a dense, pensive silence in the opulent chamber, broken only by the resolute steps of Gokhale. He was almost at the threshold, his back to the assembly, when Cyrus's voice, firm and resonant, sliced through the quiet.

"Gokhale, wait."

The two words, simple yet heavy with authority, caused Gokhale to halt mid-step, a silent command he could not ignore. He turned slowly, facing the source of the interjection, his expression a carefully neutral mask.

"Gokhale, your intention to step down strikes at the very heart of our political theatre," he began, his voice resonant and steady. "Facing you across the electoral battlefield would not just be an honour, it would also be a crucible of my political mettle."

Gokhale, who had been on the cusp of exit, paused, the air around him hanging heavy with the significance of Cyrus's words. Cyrus stepped forward, his presence commanding the room. "You wield the support of the RSD, a behemoth of social influence, and you stand with the weathered wisdom of many years," Cyrus continued, the room hanging on to every word. "In contrast, I stand somewhat isolated, my political lineage not buttressed by such cadres or history. It draws a parallel, does it not, to the legendary Mahabharata? Where Arjuna, mighty though he was, had only Lord Krishna at his chariot's reigns. Now, it seems my guiding force chooses to depart."

Cyrus's words struck a chord, and the narrative of the Mahabharata hung between them, a poignant metaphor for the impending struggle.

Gokhale's eyes sparkled with the fire of unspoken stories, his smile slow to form but impossible to ignore. He faced Cyrus with the composure of a seasoned sage. "The RSD shall remain as it has always been, a vanguard for societal upliftment, not a pawn in the political chessboard," he pronounced with unwavering certainty. "Rest assured, Cyrus, should I choose to stand in opposition, I will do so stripped of all but my conviction. For the essence of a true contest," he concluded, with the faintest tremor of anticipation, "is in the balance of forces, not the might of one over another."

The two leaders, despite their differences, shared a moment of understanding. The nation they both loved was ever-evolving, and it was up to them to guide it with respect, understanding, and unity.

Cyrus turned to Dr. Dharmadhikari. "Dr. Dharmadhikari," he began, his voice carrying a mix of regret and resolve, "I'm afraid we'll have to postpone our meeting. Gokhale's resignation has created a situation that requires my immediate attention."

Dr. Dharmadhikari, sensing the gravity of the moment, nodded in understanding. "Of course, Prime Minister," he replied, his tone reflecting his respect for the office and the man who held it. "These are indeed pressing times, and the stability of the government must be your priority. The Constitution is the foundation of our future, but it can wait until the present is secured."

Cyrus offered a weary but grateful smile. "Thank you for your understanding, Dr. Dharmadhikari. Your commitment to our nation's future is invaluable, and I assure you we will reconvene soon to continue our work on the Constitution."

Dr. Dharmadhikari bowed slightly, acknowledging the prime minister's words. "I await your call, Prime Minister. In these challenging times, my support and services are always at your disposal," he said before quietly exiting the room.

Gokhale's resignation sent shockwaves throughout the country.

With his departure, the political landscape was thrown into disarray. Cyrus was caught in a storm of his own making.

The prime minister's grand office had seen numerous discussions over the years, but this news carried a unique heaviness of anticipation. Outside the tall windows, the evening sun cast a golden hue over the national flag, its tricolour fluttering with pride.

The next morning, the atmosphere in the prime minister's office was tense and charged, a palpable sense of urgency filling the room following Gokhale's unexpected resignation. Cyrus sat behind his desk, his expression sombre, reflecting how grave the situation was. The door opened, and Panditji and Patel Sahib entered, their faces etched with concern. Seated at his expansive teak desk, Cyrus was lost in thought.

Across from him, Patel Sahib cleared his throat and began, "Cyrus, the country has come a long way under your leadership. But it's time to solidify the foundation of our democracy. It's time for fresh elections."

Panditji, leaning forward in his chair, added, "New Bharat is ready, Cyrus. Our citizens, young and old, are eager to have their voices heard. An elected leadership is the next logical step in our nation's journey."

Nair, meticulously going through some documents, looked up. "The administrative machinery is prepared. We've been working on a potential electoral process, ensuring it's transparent and inclusive."

Cyrus took a moment, absorbing the weight of the proposition. "It's not about me, or any individual for that matter. It's about New Bharat's future," he mused aloud. "Announcing fresh elections… it's the right thing to do."

Patel Sahib nodded in agreement. "It'll be a testament to our commitment to democracy. The world is watching, and our people are waiting."

Cyrus was still reeling from Gokhale's resignation. Panditji put forward a proposal that could alter the political landscape. "Cyrus," he began, his voice steady and imbued with a sense of gravity, "after considerable discussion within our party and consultation with our members, we have reached a consensus. We believe that it's in the best interest of the Indian National Party, and indeed the nation, for you to be our nominee in the upcoming elections."

Cyrus, taken aback by the proposition, looked from Panditji to Patel Sahib, searching their faces for signs of the reasoning behind this unexpected turn. Patel Sahib, usually more reticent, added in his deep, resonant voice, "Cyrus, this decision wasn't made lightly. We've observed your leadership, your ability to handle crises, and most importantly, your commitment to the unity and progress of our nation. Despite our initial reservations, we now believe you are the best candidate to lead not only our party but the country forward."

The room fell silent as Cyrus absorbed the implications of their words. To be the nominee of the Indian National Party was an immense responsibility, one that came with both challenges and opportunities. He realized the proposal was evidence of the trust and confidence they had in his leadership, despite his initial outsider status in the realm of politics.

"I am honoured by your trust," Cyrus finally spoke, his voice reflecting the solemnity of the moment. "But this is a significant shift from my position as an interim prime minister. How do you foresee this affecting the party dynamics and the public perception?"

Panditji exchanged a glance with Patel Sahib before responding. "We've deliberated over this extensively. The party members respect your neutrality and your dedication to national interests above partisan politics. Your candidacy would symbolize a new era for the Indian National Party, one that transcends traditional political boundaries."

Patel Sahib nodded in agreement. "Moreover, your leadership during these turbulent times has garnered public admiration. You've demonstrated a balance of pragmatism and vision that resonates with the people. We believe your candidacy will not only unify our party but also appeal to the wider electorate."

Cyrus listened intently, understanding the implications of their request. This was more than a political strategy; it was an opportunity to steer the nation's course towards a future he envisioned — united, progressive, and strong.

Taking a deep breath, Cyrus made his decision. "If my candidacy serves the best interests of our nation and the party, then I accept your proposal. It's time for us to prepare for the elections and work together towards a victory for the Indian National Party and for India."

As the meeting concluded, Panditji and Patel Sahib left with a sense of accomplishment while Cyrus sat back, contemplating the journey ahead. The road to the elections would be challenging, but he was ready to face it with the support of the Indian National Party, armed with a vision for a new India.

November 20, 1952:
The Prime Minister's Office

It was a chilly day in Delhi when Prime Minister Engineer, seated in his imposing study, called upon representatives from all political factions of the nation. The formidable task ahead was to set up the very foundation of India's burgeoning democracy: the Election Commission.

The room was filled with a myriad of personalities, each with their own vision for the future of India. From leftists to right-wingers, regional champions to national stalwarts, the spectrum of India's political diversity was present in that room.

The air was thick with scepticism. Many wondered if they could ever reach a consensus. After all, political adversaries were expected to come together and form a neutral entity that would oversee the world's largest democratic exercise.

"Thank you all for coming," Cyrus began, scanning the room. "Today, we are not representatives of individual parties. Today, we represent the idea of India. Our goal is to ensure that every citizen, irrespective of caste, creed, or religion, gets a fair chance to voice their opinion."

There was a brief pause, as if the room collectively caught its breath.

Hamid was the first to respond, "Mr. Prime Minister, while your sentiment is commendable, let's be realistic. How do we ensure that this commission remains impartial?"

Cyrus, always the tactician, replied, "By ensuring that its creation is a combined effort. Each of you will nominate a member who you believe embodies the principles of fairness and neutrality. Together, they will form the core of the Election Commission."

There were murmurs of agreement, but Hamid, always cynical, voiced the concern on everyone's mind. "And who will lead this commission?"

Mr. Nair, with his characteristic wit, quipped from the corner, "Someone who can handle all of you, of course!" The room erupted in laughter, lightening the tense atmosphere.

Cyrus took this opportunity to steer the conversation. "The head of the commission will be someone outside of our political sphere. An individual respected by all, untouched by biases. We'll collectively decide on that."

As hours turned into days, the group delved into the intricacies of the mammoth task ahead. Logistics, voting methods, booth security, voter registration—every aspect was discussed, debated, and finalized.

It was during these discussions that a blueprint for India's democratic future was drawn. The Election Commission, a beacon of hope and fairness, was conceived from the collective vision of diverse minds.

News of the impending elections created a buzz in every nook and corner of India. Gokhale, harnessing his vast networks and using the issue of secularism as his plank, formed a new political outfit.

The atmosphere across New Bharat in December was electric. Though winter had cast its cold fingers over much of the country, the political fervour generated warmth, noise, and excitement that was unmistakable.

In Nagpur, a sea of people, many with faces painted and holding banners, had turned up to see Gokhale, the man who had defied expectations and formed his own political outfit. As Gokhale took the stage, there was a hush followed by an overwhelming cheer. His voice, filled with passion and conviction, echoed through the speakers. "New Bharat is at a crossroads. We stand on the edge of carving our own destiny. It is time to look beyond political affiliations and focus on development, unity, and prosperity. The legacy of the past cannot be our future."

Further north, in the historical city of Lucknow, Hamid had drawn an impressive crowd. Flags with the emblem of the Muslim Quam flapped in the winter breeze. "It is not about religion or race," Hamid declared. "It's about the dreams and aspirations of every citizen of New Bharat. The Muslim Quam seeks a harmonious coexistence, a shared dream, and equal opportunities for everyone."

Meanwhile, in the bustling streets of Calcutta, Sunita Bose, leader of the Progressive Unity Party, drew her audience with tales of India's past glories and the promise of a socialist future. "We have been merchants, kings, scholars, and saints. It's time we reclaim our legacy and build a society based on equity, education, and empowerment."

Down south, in Madras, Rajan Naidu of the National Reform Party captured imaginations with a vision of a technologically advanced New Bharat. "Innovation, science, and technology will be our new scriptures. Our young minds are our biggest assets, and it's time to invest in them."

Contrasting the political fervour, in a quaint café in Bombay, young intellectuals and college students gathered to meet Cyrus. The walls, adorned with posters of revolutionaries and poets, set the mood. Here, in an informal setting, Cyrus was scheduled to meet some of the brightest young minds from colleges across New Bharat.

The anticipation in the air was intense as the selected students, representing diverse fields of study, waited for the prime minister. Conversations among them were animated, their youth bubbling with questions, concerns, and hopes for the future of their newly formed nation.

Varun, a literature student, mused, "These rallies, the speeches… they talk of a future, but how inclusive is this future? What's the roadmap?"

Ananya, an economics major, countered, "It's a start. For the first time, we're seeing leaders emerge from the grassroots, talking about development and not just politics."

Varun, continued, "Sir, we hear a lot about unity and development in political speeches. But as a nation with such rich diversity, how do we ensure that no one is left behind?"

Ananya, the economics major, added, "Our economy is at a crossroads. We have the potential to become a global powerhouse, but our policies need to focus on innovation and inclusivity. We need a roadmap."

Rajat, an engineering student from Chennai, emphasized the importance of investing in technology and research. "We have the minds and the talent. But there's a lack of infrastructure and opportunities."

Cyrus listened intently, nodding occasionally. "Your concerns are valid. This is precisely why we need young leaders like you to step up. New Bharat isn't just about the decisions made in the corridors of power. It's about each citizen, each idea, each dream. And while we'll have our challenges, with the energy and passion I see here, I'm optimistic."

Their exchange carried on as the fading sun cloaked the gardens in a luminous, apricot-tinted light, heralding the evening's arrival. By the time it ended, there was a renewed sense of purpose among the students. And for Cyrus, it was a reminder that the heart of New Bharat lay in its youth, its future leaders.

And so, as 1952 drew to a close, it was clear that New Bharat was on the brink of change. A change fuelled by aspirations and the indomitable spirit of its people. The winds of change were blowing, and they carried with them the promise of a new dawn.

It was a historic moment for India, a monumental turning point. After gaining independence, the nation was embracing democracy with open arms, preparing for its very first general election. Alliances were forged overnight, manifestos were printed and distributed like hotcakes, and promises—some genuine, some not—were being made.

Lines snaked around polling booths as people of all ages, backgrounds, and professions waited patiently to cast their votes. The enthusiasm was contagious; elderly citizens, supported by their grandchildren, made their way to the booths, determined to be a part of this momentous occasion. Women in colourful sarees, men in crisp kurtas, and young adults sporting badges and wristbands of their chosen party created a mosaic of colours and voices.

International reporters thronged the streets, their cameras rolling continuously. "We're here in Delhi, witnessing history," one of them announced, "as millions come together to participate in the largest democratic exercise ever seen!"

Three Months Later: Cyrus's Residence, Bombay

In the subdued glow of candlelight, Cyrus's mansion in Bombay took on an almost ethereal quality. The earthquake's tremors had long since subsided, but their aftershocks reverberated through the power grid, leaving parts of the city cloaked in an involuntary return to simpler times. Despite the modernity that usually illuminated every corner of his palatial home, tonight it was awash with the flickering dance of candle flames, casting long, quivering shadows against the walls.

The evening was doused in a sort of restless anticipation. The first election results of independent India would be announced in a matter of minutes. The low hum of a radio filled the prime minister's residence, interspersed with the occasional static.

Outside, a gusty wind was blowing, and the curtains inside fluttered, occasionally letting in cold gusts that made the candle flames dance. A storm was brewing, both outside and within the walls of the residence.

However, inside the luxuriant room, the warm ochre hue of the setting sun filtered through the tall, arched windows. There, amidst the stacks of important documents, memos, and communications that bore testament to the tumultuous birth of a new nation, lay a single parchment of great significance: 'The Constitution of India'.

The crisp, off-white paper stood out. Its elegance was captivating, promising a fresh slate for millions. But there, on one of its opening pages, the word 'Secular' was circled in bold red, and beside it, a small question mark.

It was a question left unanswered, hinting at the delicate balance of a diverse nation. A question about the course this new country would take in the years ahead. Would it remain true to the spirit of its inception, or would it waver in the face of challenges?

At the centre, a chessboard was laid out on a mahogany table, a silent battleground of black-and-white squares. Across from Cyrus sat a mysterious figure, his features softened by the candlelight's gentle touch, rendering him an enigmatic presence.

This man, whose identity was obscured by the muted lighting, moved his chess pieces with a deliberate, almost ceremonial precision.

Cyrus, meanwhile, was lost in contemplation. His fingers hovered over a knight, contemplating its journey across the checkered landscape. The air was heavy with the scent of beeswax and the faintest hint of sandalwood, a sensory echo of tradition amidst the calm of concentration.

The silence was punctuated only by the distant sound of a radio, its voice crackling through the air, announcing the results of the elections.

Unmoved by the broadcast, Cyrus's opponent simply sat, an inscrutable smile playing on his lips, as if the real game was here, on this board between them. The radio's voice became a distant murmur, like the waves of the Arabian Sea lapping at the edges of consciousness.

The deep, solemn chimes of a grandfather clock echoed through the room. It was almost time for the radio announcement. Cyrus's eyes were sharp, focused, studying every move, every possibility. Opposite him, the tall, enigmatic man looked on with an equally keen intensity.

Each move was met with silence, the only sound being the methodical ticking of the clock and the soft clinks of the chess pieces. The game had been on for hours, and the tension between the players was like an electric current.

Suddenly, Cyrus made his move, and in a soft, calculated voice, whispered, "Checkmate."

Maharaja Rajyavardhan looked stunned. He glanced down at the board, realizing his king was trapped. As he looked up, the radio static broke the tension.

"... and ladies and gentlemen, history has been made! Cyrus is declared the prime minister in independent India's first-ever election!"

As the words sunk in, Rajyavardhan's gaze shifted from the board to Cyrus. "Two victories in one night, Mr. Prime Minister. Impressive."

Cyrus gave a tight-lipped smile. Before he could reply, a gust of wind blew open the windows, extinguishing the candles and throwing the room into darkness. Rajyavardhan stood up abruptly, the chair scraping loudly against the floor.

Without saying a word, Cyrus stood up, the import of his victory evident in his expression. He walked over to his library, selected a book, and immersed himself in its pages. It was a classic move from Cyrus, seeking solace and wisdom in literature during times of immense pressure.

Maharaja Rajyavardhan, meanwhile, took a moment to observe the room, his eyes landing on a neatly folded piece of paper peeking from under the chessboard. It was a telegram. Pulling it out, he read aloud, "Thank you for all you've done. Warm regards, Prime Minister of Israel."

The storm outside seemed to echo the storm inside Rajyavardhan's mind. Cyrus, with his ever-calm demeanour, took a deep breath. "Every move, every decision, Maharaja, has its consequences. Some play for the game, some for the endgame."

Rajyavardhan's eyebrows furrowed, questions brewing in his mind. He looked towards Cyrus, who continued to read, his face impassive.

The chessboard was laid out, each piece intricately carved, each with a story to tell. The game seemed completed, yet no one could ascertain which move had actually sealed the game.

Cyrus stood by the window, gazing out into the night, a Cuban cigar smouldering between his fingers. The room was steeped in silence, save for the distant hum of the bustling city. A smirk played on his lips as he pondered over the chessboard of political manoeuvring that had led to his landslide victory in the elections.

Cyrus mulled his thoughts, swirling as much as the smoke from his cigar. Was it the removal of Hamid, he wondered, that had been the game changer? The move had undoubtedly secured the Hindu votes, which had been on edge with a Muslim finance minister. Cyrus recalled the secret message sent by him to the US president, facilitating a covert meeting between Hamid and a CIA operative. Was this tactical play the one that turned the tides in his favour? Hamid, once a trusted ally, had begun to cast a long shadow, one that loomed over Cyrus's own stature in the political arena. In the chess game of politics, Hamid was becoming a king in his own right, a potential challenger in the next election—a challenge Cyrus could ill afford. Hamid's decision to communicate the execution of the spy to his Russian counterparts had been a misstep, a self-goal in the intricate game of political football. It was an opportunity Cyrus recognized he had to exploit but with the finesse of a chess grandmaster. The move had to be precise, calculated to sideline Hamid without raising suspicion over Cyrus's own intentions. Cyrus pondered the strategy. Hamid's growing ambition and his clandestine meeting had given him the ammunition he needed, but the execution had to be flawless. Hamid had to emerge as the villain in this political drama while he, Cyrus, had to be seen as the unwitting victim, a leader betrayed by his own finance minister's overreaching ambitions. The narrative had to be tight, with no loose ends that could point back to Cyrus orchestrating the downfall. Hamid's unwitting self-goal had presented him with a golden opportunity, one that he would exploit to its fullest to ensure his continued reign at the helm of the nation's affairs.

Or perhaps it was Gokhale's well-orchestrated resignation that sealed the deal for him, Cyrus mused. It was a move that had the potential to rally the Muslim votes back to his side, votes that had been alienated by Hamid's dismissal. And then there was the masterstroke of insisting on adding the word 'secular' in the preamble of the Constitution. Cyrus dwelled on that point, his thoughts tracing the sophisticated web of political strategy that had led to this moment. Sidestepping Gokhale had been one of the most challenging moves. Gokhale, with his vast network and deep-rooted ethos, was not just an ally; he was a formidable presence in the political landscape. Cyrus knew the depth of Gokhale's commitment to his principles, a commitment that was both an asset and a hurdle. The key lay in the preamble of the Constitution— specifically, the inclusion of the word 'secular.' This wasn't in the original draft, but Cyrus had sensed an opportunity there. It was a subtle yet potent trigger, one he knew would resonate deeply with Gokhale's convictions. Gokhale's resignation, while a difficult pill to swallow, had been a necessary step in Cyrus's path to maintain his grip on power. It was a move that would create ripples, altering the political dynamics in his favour. Cyrus had anticipated resistance, possibly even a backlash, but Gokhale's departure from the cabinet had smoothed the path considerably. Yet, what truly sealed the deal was Gokhale's assurance that he wouldn't seek the support of the RSD in contesting the elections. That promise was the cherry on top of the cake, the final piece that solidified Cyrus's position. It ensured that Gokhale, despite his influence and following, would not pose a significant threat to Cyrus's campaign. As Cyrus sat there, a plan taking shape in his mind, he couldn't help but marvel at the complexity of the political chess game he was engaged in. Gokhale's resignation, spurred by the strategic placement of 'secular' in the Constitution's preamble, had been a masterstroke, albeit a risky one. It was a move that demonstrated the delicate balance of power, persuasion, and principle. In the grand scheme of things, it had cleared the way for Cyrus, ensuring his unchallenged ascendancy in the tumultuous arena of politics.

Then there was the possibility that his nomination as the PM candidate for the Indian National Party was the final, decisive move. With Panditji and Patel Sahib both strong contenders, neither wanting the other in the spotlight, Cyrus had emerged as the natural choice. It was a move that had effectively sidelined two of the most influential figures in the party. In a game where power was the ultimate prize, had the towering egos of Panditji and Patel Sahib inadvertently handed him the board? He chuckled softly, the sound echoing in the quiet room. The very thought that these two political titans, each a force in their own right, might have unwittingly paved his path to victory was both ironic and thrilling. Their rivalry, so entrenched and visible, had created a unique vacuum, a space that only he could fill. Did their desire to thwart each other's ambitions lead to his unexpected rise? In their chess game of political manoeuvrers, had Panditji and Patel Sahib unwittingly checkmated themselves? Had their request for him to run on behalf of the Indian National Party, instead of as an independent, been the unwitting endorsement he needed to rally the entire party—and the nation—behind him? Cyrus took another puff of his cigar, the smoke a metaphor for the murky waters of political strategy. In the quiet of the night, with the city's heartbeat pulsing in the distance, Cyrus realized the irony of his triumph. It was a victory born not just from his own strategic plays but from the very rivalry that was meant to keep him in check. The game had indeed been thrilling, the outcome spectacular, and the realization that he might owe his victory to the egos of two political giants was a twist that even he hadn't anticipated.

But Cyrus couldn't discount the behind-the-scenes understanding with Maharaja Rajyavardhan and the other seventeen princes. By guaranteeing them privy purses, he had secured the allegiance of their subjects, a significant block of votes that could have easily swayed the election results. He knew all too well that his electoral victory wouldn't have been complete without the support of Maharaja Rajyavardhan. The announcement of privy purses to the rulers had been a tactical move, one that turned the erstwhile rulers into allies, but Cyrus was acutely aware of the underlying complexities. These princes and maharajas weren't just figureheads; they commanded loyalty and reverence from their subjects, loyalty that had been nurtured and strengthened over generations. Their support was not just a political convenience; it was a necessity, a bridge to the hearts and minds of countless citizens who still looked up to their traditional leaders. Bringing Maharaja Rajyavardhan back from exile had been a crucial part of his strategy. Rajyavardhan wasn't just another ruler; he was a symbol, a unifying figure whose influence extended far beyond his own domain. His exile had created a void, and his return was a statement, a signal to the other rulers and their subjects that a new era of cooperation and unity under Cyrus's leadership was beginning. Cyrus pondered over the delicate negotiations, the careful weaving of assurances and respect that had brought Rajyavardhan, and subsequently, the other rulers to his side. It was a dance of diplomacy and promise, where the past was acknowledged and a future was forged together. In the grand chessboard of political manoeuvring, Maharaja Rajyavardhan's support was a king-making move. It wasn't just about securing the blessings of the rulers; it was about winning the hearts of their subjects. Cyrus's decision to secure this support, to bridge the divide between the old world and the new, was an indication of his understanding of the nuanced fabric of Indian society. In this chess game, Rajyavardhan was more than a bishop or a knight; he was a crucial kingmaker, his moves essential to Cyrus's ultimate checkmate.

Cyrus wondered, was it his instruction to Nalini to meet Israel's prime minister—promising India's support for a Jewish state at the UN General Assembly in exchange for Israeli investment in agriculture—that ultimately swayed the election a redefining point? This strategic move, executed with precision and shrouded in secrecy, may have been the masterstroke that secured the critical farmer vote. By aligning India with Israel, Cyrus not only showcased his diplomatic acumen but also potentially unlocked the support of a key demographic, thus tipping the electoral scales in his favour. It was a calculated gamble aimed at a demographic that could sway the electoral outcome. The farmers, long the backbone of the nation, were a segment whose support was pivotal. The promise of a revolution in agricultural practices, backed by Israeli technology and investment, could have been the key that unlocked their support for Cyrus.

It was a complex game of chess, played on a board that spanned the breadth of a nation teetering on the brink of division. Ali Bhai had made a calculated move, appointing Hamid as the second most powerful minister in the government. It was a strategic placement that served multiple purposes. Not only did it ensure representation of the Muslim Quam in the highest echelons of power, but it also cornered the British Empire, preventing them from using India as a mere pawn in their larger political interests. On the other side of the board, Panditji and Patel Sahib manoeuvred with equal finesse. They used Cyrus, a young and relatively inexperienced leader, to avoid the partition of India and to keep the Muslim Quam from gaining outright power. They banked on Cyrus's loyalty and respect for his father, a known advisor of their party, and they were confident that his inexperience would make him reliant on their guidance and counsel.

But the true act of genius came from Cyrus himself. Initially perceived as a passive player, a mere figurehead chosen for his neutrality, Cyrus's journey was marked by an evolving understanding of the political landscape and his role within it. He outplayed those who sought to use him as a tool for their own agendas. His final moves on the political chessboard were a testament to his growth from a reluctant leader to a master strategist. His ambition, often overshadowed by his apparent niceness and inexperience, became his most powerful weapon. As he traversed the tumultuous waters of Indian politics, making alliances and decisions that often surprised those around him, it became evident that Cyrus was not just a participant in this game but a formidable player.

As Cyrus took a slow drag of his cigar, the smoke swirling around him like the mysteries of his campaign, he knew that the true game changer might never be revealed. Each move had been calculated, each decision weighed for its potential impact. But which one had truly sealed his victory was a secret that the night would keep.

The smirk widened as he turned away from the window, the game won but the mystery of his triumph remaining, like the cigar's smoke, an elusive, drifting enigma.

The game of chess is as much about the players as it is about the pieces. Every move, every strategy is a reflection of the player's intent, and in the vast game of politics and power, the lines between player and pawn often blur.

Much like a tale spun by Watson from the notes of Sherlock Holmes, the true narrative was cryptic, full of red herrings, and clouded in intrigue. Every piece, every player, had a tale, but the true story, the grand design, remained tantalizingly out of reach.

The journey of Cyrus as prime minister had been a tumultuous one, marked by a blend of challenges and triumphs. He had navigated the multifaceted political waters with a deft hand, but there was an unspoken truth that lingered in the air—much of his path had been set for him, the power handed to him on a platter through a series of calculated moves and fortunate circumstances. Yet, the real challenge lay ahead, in the uncharted waters of a post-election India, where his leadership would be truly tested.

The next day, as Cyrus sat in his office, the early morning light filtering through the windows, his gaze fell upon the day's newspaper. The bold headline captured his attention: 'King Farouk of Egypt is ousted by a military coup'. The news was a stark reminder of the volatility of power and the ever-changing dynamics of leadership. It was a world where thrones could crumble and crowns could fall in the blink of an eye.

He leaned back in his chair, his mind racing with thoughts of the future. The past few years had been a game of chess, where he had moved his pieces with strategic precision. But now, as he stood at the threshold of a new era, he wondered if the next chapter of his journey would be another chessboard, where strategy and foresight would guide his moves, or a *chakravyuh*, an elaborate and inescapable web of challenges and dilemmas.

The uncertainty of what lay ahead was both daunting and exhilarating. Cyrus knew that the road ahead would require more than political acumen; it would demand resilience, adaptability, and, above all, a vision for the nation that transcended mere politics.

As he prepared himself for the challenges ahead, Cyrus realized that the true test of his leadership had just begun. Would he emerge victorious, navigating the convoluted labyrinth of governance and diplomacy, or would the *chakravyuh* of political intrigue and unforeseen challenges ensnare him? The future was unwritten, the story of Bharat was just beginning, and whispers hinted that another chapter awaited.

www.ingramcontent.com/pod-product-compliance
Lightning Source LLC
Chambersburg PA
CBHW031121160726

47989CB00016B/81